"Drop your pants, Sergeant."

Ray Darling looked over his shoulder and grinned. "Well, Nurse Pritchard. I didn't know you cared."

The nurse tried not to smile, but Ray could see that the corners of her mouth had begun to twitch. Still, she did have that hypodermic needle in her hand.

So Sergeant Darling sucked it in and did as he was told. Getting a gamma globulin shot because somebody who worked in the base snack bar had contracted hepatitis B was bad enough, but having the "Ice Princess Nurse," Prickly Pritchard, give it to him made it twice as bad. It surprised him that she'd actually responded to his lame line.

Prickly Pritchard was probably the best-looking nurse in the flight surgeon's clinic. Ray was just as attracted to her as anyone else at Hurlburt Field, but more experienced men than he had tried to pierce her icy reserve and failed.

"Fire away, ma'am," he said. He was a combat controller. He was tough. He could handle one small needle.

It was worse than he expected. Ray bit back a groan as the serum went in. He couldn't help wondering if Prickly Pritchard got her thrills out of inflicting pain.

"Pull 'em up, Sergeant. I'm finished," Nurse Pritchard said. "You can go."

Dear Reader,

I've read so many romances that portray military men as rough, tough caricatures that I felt I had to write about the wonderful, three-dimensional men I had a chance to know when I was growing up as an army brat, and as an adult with an air force husband. Sure, these men are physically fit and trained in weapons and covert techniques, but they have hearts and minds and feelings, as well.

Most of these guys can certainly assault a building with guns in both hands if they have to, but more often they are Little League coaches and Boy Scout leaders. They eat MREs (Meal, Ready to Eat) if they have to, but they can also grill a steak and toss together an omelet. If they have any shortcoming, it's that they fall in love too hard, and too fast.

Ray Darling is one of those guys, and he has to work hard to get Prickly Patsy Pritchard to give him a second glance. When she finally does, it's magic. I hope you'll love Ray (Radar) Darling as much as Patsy and I do.

Fondly,

Bonnie Gardner

Books by Bonnie Gardner

HARLEQUIN AMERICAN ROMANCE

876—UNCLE SARGE
911—SGT. BILLY'S BRIDE
958—THE SERGEANT'S SECRET SON
970—PRICELESS MARRIAGE

SERGEANT DARLING
Bonnie Gardner

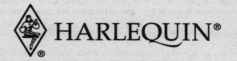

TORONTO • NEW YORK • LONDON
AMSTERDAM • PARIS • SYDNEY • HAMBURG
STOCKHOLM • ATHENS • TOKYO • MILAN • MADRID
PRAGUE • WARSAW • BUDAPEST • AUCKLAND

ISBN 0-373-75023-4

SERGEANT DARLING

www.eHarlequin.com

Printed in U.S.A.

To Mud, as always.

To all the men who've had to leave their women behind
to fight for their country, and all the women
who waited at home with yellow ribbons
on their mailboxes and in their hair.

Chapter One

"Drop your pants, Sergeant."

Ray Darling looked over his shoulder and grinned. "Well, Nurse Pritchard. I didn't know you cared."

The nurse tried not to smile, but Ray could see that the corners of her mouth had begun to twitch. Still, she did have that hypodermic needle in her hand.

So Sergeant Darling sucked it in and did as he was told. It was bad enough to have to submit to getting a gamma globulin shot because somebody who worked in the base snack bar had contracted hepatitis B, but to have the "Ice Princess Nurse," Prickly Pritchard, give it to him made it twice as bad. It surprised him that she'd actually responded to his lame line.

Prickly Pritchard was probably the best-looking nurse in the Flight Surgeon's Clinic at Hurlburt

Field, near Fort Walton Beach on the northern panhandle of Florida. She had a curvy figure that could
put any underwear model to shame, blond hair, blue
eyes and flawless skin. Unfortunately, the good
nurse was as prickly as a cactus. Not that that
seemed to matter to the servicemen who came to
her clinic. Her signature rebuffs to anyone who
showed the slightest attraction to her only succeeded in fanning the flames of interest and spec-
ulation by every red-blooded male on base.

Ray was just as attracted to her as anyone else
on Hurlburt, but more experienced men than he had
tried to get through her icy reserve and failed, so
he had never tried. It sure would be a big boost to
his ego if Ray were able to get to first base when
the hotshot aviator types who believed they were
God's gifts to women hadn't been able to melt
through her icy shield.

It was worth a try. Just not today.

He might be an excellent sergeant after ten years
in the air force, but he still hadn't perfected his
social skills. That had been one of the drawbacks
of being a ''boy genius,'' something he'd done his
best to conceal when he'd enlisted, mostly by keeping his mouth shut to keep his larger-than-average
vocabulary from being apparent.

Twelve-year-olds in high school didn't date, and
when he'd enrolled in college at fourteen, he hadn't

had much time to try. And when he had, he'd struck out with the older women in his classes. After a while, he'd just quit trying.

And after he'd defied his parents and joined the air force instead of going on to graduate school at eighteen, he'd spent so much of his time learning how to be a good sergeant and trying to be a "regular guy" that dating hadn't been a priority. Now at twenty-eight, he wished he'd had as much training in that particular area as he'd had in all things air force. Unfortunately, no book taught that particular skill. Not in any useful way, anyway. Although, the tired old line he'd heard in the movies had seemed to put a tiny dent in Nurse Pritchard's armor.

"Fire away, ma'am," he said, flinching as he felt the swipe from the alcohol wipe and steeled himself for the jab of the needle. He was a combat controller. He was tough. He could handle one small needle.

It was worse than he'd expected. Ray bit back a groan of pain as the serum went in. Damn. He'd thought he was prepared for it, but this was nowhere close to what he'd expected. He couldn't help wondering if Prickly Pritchard got her thrills out of inflicting pain.

"Pull 'em up, Sergeant Darling, I'm finished," Nurse Pritchard said, her tone all business. "You'll be sore, but you'll live. You can go."

Ray half expected her to slap him on his butt, but thankfully, she didn't. Figuring now wasn't the best time to try anything with her, Ray pulled up his trousers and made a rapid exit.

He wasn't really beating a hasty retreat. He'd been summoned by his commanding officer, for what he didn't know, and he didn't have time to hang around and trade shots with Pritchard, even if he thought he'd gotten in a couple of points with that twitch of a smile. She'd already won anyway, he thought with a wry smile, and resisted the urge to rub his rump, as he strode away.

"You know, that one's pretty cute, Patsy," Senior Airman Nancy Oakley, the receptionist, commented to Nurse Pritchard as she stepped into the waiting room to call her next patient. "If I didn't have my own personal sweetie, I might give him a run for his money," she continued, patting her pregnant stomach.

"I'm sure Andy would love to hear that," Patsy said with a smile. Nancy was right, though. Sergeant Darling was as cute as his name. No, he wasn't cute, he was downright gorgeous. "And you know my rule about not getting involved with men that come through the clinic, so that leaves both of us out," she added as she considered the man who'd just left the examination room.

The sergeant certainly qualified as tall, dark and handsome, in spite of the thick plastic government issue glasses he wore. The guys called them B.C., for birth control, because they were so darned ugly. But even with the glasses, or maybe in spite of them, Ray Darling could turn heads. And if Ray Darling could turn hers, he could turn anyone's.

"You know, he'd really look great if he'd take off the glasses," Nancy said, handing Patsy the file for her next patient.

Patsy laughed. "Funny, I was just thinking the same thing. But then the glasses work for him. They make him look smart and kind instead of dangerous like some of the other guys he works with. And I think he really is different from those macho bruisers in the special operations squadron. He's always so quiet and polite when he comes into the clinic."

"Yeah, I like that tongue-tied, shy-with-girls kind'a thing," Nancy said. "And the glasses do nothing to disguise that square jaw."

"So true," Patsy agreed, thinking less about Sergeant Darling's jaw than his broad back, narrow waist and well-shaped buns, which she'd seen at close quarters. And if Sergeant Darling's little quip was any indication, he'd started getting over his shyness. And she rather liked that.

Not that it made much difference.

She didn't have to worry about Sergeant Darling

or any of the other men assigned to Hurlburt Field making passes at her. She'd rebuffed so many advances from men who came through the clinic that only the worst egomaniacs kept asking. Sometimes she wished the others would persist, too.

Patsy drew in a deep breath, or maybe it was a sigh. Today, because of her brief exchange with Sergeant Darling, was one of those times.

RED BERET IN HAND, Ray rapped on the jamb of Colonel John Harbeson's open office door before stepping inside. "You wanted to see me, sir?" he asked when the colonel looked up.

Harbeson beckoned Ray inside. "No, Radar," he clarified, then he smiled. "Actually, my wife wants to speak to you."

Ray winced at the nickname he hated, but he wasn't about to correct his commanding officer, and it sure beat "Darling," which some of the guys had tried to tack onto him when he'd been new to combat control. It *was* his name, but still…

Once inside, he could see that the colonel wasn't alone. He hadn't noticed Mrs. Harbeson sitting on the long couch that took up most of the wall just inside the door. "I'm sorry, ma'am," he said as he folded his beret and stuck it into one of the many pockets on the legs of his uniform. "I didn't see you there."

He couldn't imagine what she could possibly want to see him about. "What can I do for you, ma'am?"

"Please, Radar, call me Marianne. I'm not your commanding officer," she said, gesturing for Ray to sit beside her. "John is."

"Yes, m— I mean, Mrs. H— I mean, Marianne." That had been hard. Mrs. Harbeson was closer to the age of his mother than any of his friends. "If you don't mind, I'd rather stand." To reinforce his statement, Ray settled into the parade rest stance, infinitely more comfortable than sitting would have been today. After all, he'd just had an injection in his keister.

"Suit yourself," Mrs. Harbeson said. "I suppose you're wondering what I could possibly want from you."

Ray nodded. "Yes, ma'am."

Mrs. Harbeson arched a well-shaped eyebrow at the *ma'am,* but she didn't correct him again. "I have a favor to ask of you."

Ray blinked. "Yes, ma'am. What can I do for you?"

She raised her hands in a gesture of surrender. "I give up."

"Ma'am?"

"Call me anything you want, Radar. Just don't call me sir."

"No, ma'am." Ray wished Mrs. Harbeson would just get on with it.

Smiling, she said, "My women's club is holding a bachelor auction to raise money for an addition to the enlisted widows' home, and I was hoping that you'd agree to be one of the bachelors we could auction off."

"Excuse me?"

He could not have heard her right. She wanted him to be auctioned off? No, that was not possible. Why would anyone want to spend good money on him? Even for charity. He was, now, and always had been, a quiet, smart guy. Not quite a geek, but close enough. Hell, he even wore glasses. He'd heard about the kinds of guys they used for those charity things. They were celebrities, hunks. Hell, they knew the right things to say in those kinds of situations. They knew how to talk to women. He was more comfortable programming a computer.

"You heard me, Radar. I want you to be one of our eligible bachelors. You are eligible, aren't you? You haven't gotten engaged or married since we chatted at the Christmas party last year, have you? You aren't going out with anyone special?"

"No, ma'am," Ray said, still shocked by the woman's request. "Are you sure you want *me?*" There had been quite a marriage boom in his squadron recently, and Ray supposed that Mrs. Harbeson had been forced to scrape pretty close to the bottom of the proverbial barrel. Why else would she be asking him to participate?

Mrs. Harbeson's request had him sweating suddenly, and Ray wiped his damp hands on the legs of his BDU—his battle dress uniform. He was sweating because he was actually seriously considering accepting. Maybe the shot he'd had earlier had affected his brain.

"Yes, Radar," Mrs. Harbeson said. "I think you'd be perfect for this assignment."

Considering that a request from his commander's wife was as good as an order from her husband, he'd best accept, he thought. Even if it was against his better judgment. Besides, he might actually meet someone interesting.

Yeah, right.

"All right, ma'am. You've got your bachelor." Ray turned to the colonel who had been strangely silent during this weird conversation. "Do you need me for anything else, sir?"

The colonel grinned. "Nothing, Ray. Marianne will fill you in on the details later. Thanks."

Ray stepped out of the office.

"Oh, and Radar," the colonel called. "Send Sergeant Murphey in to see me."

"Yes, sir," Ray said. And he promptly hurried

out to find his buddy Danny Murphey, who, apparently, was about to get pressed into service as well.

"I DON'T CARE if you do have two tickets, Aunt Myrt. I will not participate in that disgusting example of sexism," Patsy Pritchard told her aunt emphatically as she watched Myrtle primp for the Women's Auxiliary Bachelor Auction and Dinner.

Patsy knew exactly what her Aunt Myrtle was up to, and she wasn't about to encourage her in any way. "If, or when, I decide to start dating again, I'll do it on my own terms, not because I had to buy someone to take me out."

"But, Patricia, it's been years since your husband died. A beautiful young woman like you shouldn't be sitting at home alone at night with her cats. You need to be out having fun, seeing people."

Not that again, Patsy protested to herself. Why couldn't Aunt Myrtle understand that she was perfectly happy with the way things were? "I am not a hermit. I see plenty of people every day." She paused, then went on when it looked as if Aunt Myrtle was going to object. "And I know perfectly well that when you say people, you mean men. I have a job where I see men daily. If I wanted to go out, I would not have any problems getting a date," she said archly.

Not that she wanted any. Now that men had

pretty much given up asking, she was perfectly happy with the status quo. Most of the time.

She'd had a man. She'd had a husband and a family. She wasn't ready to replace them. She and Ace had been head over heels in love, and it had been too hard to lose him. She'd become a widow at twenty-one when Ace and the kids had been killed in a traffic accident. It had been a blow she'd very nearly not gotten over. "Besides, they're your cats. I have a dog."

Myrtle positioned her red pillbox hat over her gray-and-white streaked Gibson-girl upswept bun and secured it with a hat pin. Setting the scarlet-colored ostrich plume at a jaunty angle, she glanced in the oval mirror above the table by the front door and fussed with the ruffle of her purple silk blouse. She pinched her cheeks and smacked her lips to spread her fire engine red lipstick. "I'm ready." She turned to Patsy and posed. "Are you sure you won't change your mind?"

"Not a chance. You give that other ticket to someone else."

"DAMN, I FEEL LIKE a gorilla in this monkey suit," Ray grumbled as he and Danny made last-minute adjustments to their formal "dress-mess" uniforms backstage before the auction. Thank goodness they'd been permitted to wear those rather than the tuxedos he'd heard some of the other bachelors were wearing. At least, he and Danny wouldn't look like penguins.

While Ray viewed the event as nothing short of torture, Murph actually seemed to be looking forward to it. Of course, Danny's prowess with women was legendary, and he'd even lived with a woman for a while. Ray hadn't had any such experience to fall back on. As far as he was concerned, this was worse than any military inspection he'd ever endured.

He stuck a finger under the collar of his uniform and tried to loosen it. He had opted for the clip-on version of the regulation black bow tie, but his shirt collar was still tight against his Adam's apple.

"Stop fidgeting," Mrs. Harbeson said, appearing suddenly, and Ray snapped to attention. "You look very handsome, Radar. I am so glad you wore your good glasses."

"I only wear the B.C. glasses on duty," he said.

Mrs. Harbeson smiled. "I'm happy to hear that. Now relax. Have a good time. I expect you to bring the Auxiliary a good price."

"I'll do the best I can, Mrs. H." Ray had finally relaxed enough to begin calling Mrs. Harbeson that, which she seemed to prefer to *ma'am*.

She turned to Danny. "You look handsome as

ever tonight, Danny. Will you try to get Radar to loosen up for me, though?''

Danny grinned. ''Doing my best, Marianne. But you have to know that I'm going to bring in the most money. Can't let Ray Darling outdo the Irish Don Juan.''

Someone called to Mrs. Harbeson. ''I'll keep that in mind,'' she said. Chuckling to herself, she hurried away to see what the other woman wanted.

''What say, Radar? You think you'll do better than me in this auction?''

''Don't know, but are you interested in making a friendly little bet?'' One that Ray was certain to lose. Murph was known for his way with women.

''You got it in one, my man,'' Danny said, his green Irish eyes smiling. ''Loser has to spring for a case for the team.''

''You're on. Just bear in mind that I get to pick the brew if I win.'' Ray grinned. ''And I go for the imported stuff.''

''Yeah, right,'' Danny snorted. ''You win this thing, and I'll eat my little black book.''

Ray grinned. Now, that would be worth seeing, but the chances of it happening were pretty slim, as far as Radar was concerned. He'd just be happy to get this dog-and-pony show behind him.

The lady from the local television station who'd been invited to emcee took her place at the podium to the side of the stage. Someone in the wings called for everyone to be quiet and then she directed the bachelors to the waiting area in the wings.

They'd barely found their places when the emcee announced the first bachelor. Ray breathed a sigh of relief that it wasn't he. Then he settled back to see how the other guys handled the job. He knew everything there was about infiltrating an enemy camp or setting up field communications under fire, but here he was completely out of his element.

Time dragged on. Danny went for $450, one of the higher totals, and Ray didn't hold out much hope that he'd best his buddy. Meanwhile, the suspense was killing him. He was going to be the last guy to be called out on stage!

At last he was introduced by the emcee. "And now, saving one of the best for last, give me a round of applause for Staff Sergeant Ray Darling!"

He didn't know what was worse: having to participate in this circus act, or having to go out on a date with a perfect stranger.

He was firmly convinced that any woman who had to resort to buying a date was probably a long way from being anyone he wanted to go out with…

IMPATIENTLY PRESSING on the doorbell, Patsy Pritchard stood outside her aunt's house waiting for her to answer the door. It was so like Aunt Myrtle to summon her over on a wild-goose chase when Patsy had plans for the evening. She wondered what it was this time.

She focused herself to remember that Myrtle was her only living relative, and without her aunt, she would be all alone in the world. She jabbed at the doorbell again and knocked loudly on the door for good measure. Was Aunt Myrt starting to lose her hearing?

"I'm sorry, Patsy dear," Myrtle said, her voice breathy and flustered as she opened the door. She was wearing a silly, ruffled blouse with a collar that reminded Patsy of something in a portrait of Queen Elizabeth I, but otherwise her aunt seemed to be dressed to the nines.

"Did you say we were going out?" Patsy asked, glancing down at her khaki slacks and powder blue sweater set. It was fine for a movie at home, but not for the likes of the places that Aunt Myrtle usually preferred. "Was I supposed to dress up?"

"You look lovely, dear," Aunt Myrtle said, hooking a large crocheted handbag over her arm. "Yes, we're going out to dinner at the Blue Heron."

"But that place must be thirty-five miles from here!" Patsy said with alarm. She had planned a private popcorn party and B-movie marathon at her apartment tonight. It hadn't been easy to find those old Ed Wood movies, and she had been looking forward to them.

"Pish," Aunt Myrtle said as she closed the door firmly behind her. "Those old movies aren't going anywhere." Had the woman read her mind?

"I didn't say anything about movies," Patsy protested as Aunt Myrtle steered her toward her behemoth of a car. "Why can't we go someplace in town?"

"Because we're meeting a nice, young man at the Blue Heron," Aunt Myrtle said, as she opened the driver's door of her ancient Cadillac. "And you're always staying at home watching old movies. How do you expect to meet anyone like that?"

"I don't expect to. I don't *want* to. That's why I stay at home." Suddenly, Patsy realized that Aunt Myrtle was up to something. She stopped in her tracks. She would *not* be dragged out on another one of Myrtle's arranged dates. Not only did she have zero desire to meet anyone, but Myrtle's taste in eligible men had always been deplorable.

"Oh, but you must, Patsy dear. I paid a thousand dollars for him."

"You did what? Surely, I did not hear you correctly. What could possibly have possessed you to hire an *escort!* She hadn't meant to, but Patsy had allowed her voice to go shrill with the last word.

Aunt Myrtle shook her head as she climbed inside. "Really, Patricia, you have been reading the wrong kind of literature. Or did you get that foolish idea from those old movies you're always watching?" She paused long enough to take a breath, but not long enough for Patsy to come up with a decent answer. "He's one of the bachelors from the auction. If you had gone with me, you could have had the pick of the lot. My treat!" She slid across the bench seat and pushed open the passenger door. "Instead, I had to do the choosing myself."

Patsy stood with one hand resting on the top of the pink Cadillac, closed her eyes and sighed. One thousand dollars! Even though Aunt Myrtle could easily afford it, it was still a great deal of money. Much more than Patsy could afford to squander on a night out. But Aunt Myrtle would be there with them, so it wasn't exactly like a blind date. She just hoped that Myrtle's taste in men had improved since the slope-shouldered accountant she'd fixed her up with the last time.

"I give up." Patsy couldn't believe she was really going to do this. "I can't let you have wasted all that money. I'll go, but under duress," she added emphatically. *And I won't enjoy it,* she didn't say out loud.

"Of course, dear," Aunt Myrtle said knowingly

as she started the engine. "Perhaps, you ought to get in," she shouted over the engine noise.

Heaven help her! Patsy did.

RAY WONDERED WHY Miss Carter had selected such an out-of-the-way place as he drove his new Honda CRV east along Highway 98 through the darkening countryside of the Florida Panhandle. The stunted shrubby trees and the tall, gangly pines of this part of the country looked strange to him after growing up among the majestic firs of the Pacific Northwest. But the soil here was sandy and poor and couldn't support the same sort of vegetation as his verdant and green home state of Washington.

What was so wrong with the niece that the aunt had to spend a thousand dollars for a date for her and keep her hidden from civilization? Miss Carter was strange enough. God help him if the acorn had fallen too close to the tree.

He drew in a deep breath and tried to look at the positive side of this. It would give him a chance to practice dating and not ruin his chances with someone who might actually matter. An image of Nurse Pritchard flashed through his mind. Now, that was a challenge worth taking. Sort of like scaling Mount Ranier.

He chuckled and shook the notion out of his head.

Finally, after miles of driving through nowhere, with only occasional glimpses of the Gulf of Mexico through the trees, he came upon civilization. At least, what passed for it around here. There was a cluster of condominiums and shops on one side of the road, and on the other was the regular complement of seaside villas, motels and restaurants. Finally, he spotted the Blue Heron and pulled into the crushed-oyster-shell parking lot. After parking, he checked his appearance in the rearview mirror. Satisfied, he stepped outside, then drew in a deep breath. "Well, here goes nothing," he muttered to himself, striding toward the building.

Inside, he talked to the hostess and was shown to the Carter table. Miss Carter waved as she saw him coming and he waved back, but Ray was more interested in the niece—his date.

Her back was to him, but so far, the woman didn't look too bad. She had long, wavy blond hair, worn down so that it cascaded over her shoulders, and she was wearing something in light blue. He could see that she'd caught her hair with a barrette on one side to keep it away from her face, but he still couldn't see it.

Then the woman, alerted by her aunt's cheerful waving, turned his way, and Ray froze in his tracks.

No, it couldn't be. It couldn't be possible for two women to look so much alike, and yet so different. Could this lovely vision in front of him really be…

Chapter Two

Patsy turned around and almost choked on the wine she'd just sipped. No, it couldn't be. She looked again. Dressed in charcoal-gray Dockers, a white turtleneck and a navy sport jacket to ward off the chill of a late March cold front, stood the last person she ever expected to see here. Sergeant Raymond Darling in attractive designer glasses—she didn't know why she noticed them, but she did— dominated the space between their table and the next one, seeming to suck the very oxygen out of the air.

He, bless him, seemed as shocked to see her as she was to see him.

They looked at each other, unable to draw their gazes away, until Ray swallowed. Patsy watched, fascinated as his Adam's apple bobbed.

"Sort of feels like being trapped in the headlights of a speeding train," he finally said under his breath. He hadn't really directed his comment to Patsy, but she understood that it was intended for her, and she doubted that Aunt Myrtle had heard him.

"Good evening, Miss Carter," he said to Aunt Myrtle, then he nodded toward Patsy, and she forced a tentative smile, welcoming smile.

"Good evening, Raymond. I've always appreciated promptness in a man," Myrtle Carter returned. She offered him a bejeweled hand, and Ray wasn't sure whether to kiss it or shake it. He opted for the latter.

"Yes, ma'am," Ray said, shrugging out of his jacket and draping it over the fourth chair. "I strive to be on time. The air force pretty well requires it," he added. On the way over he had told himself that the sooner he got there, the sooner this fiasco would be over and done with. Now, he wasn't so sure he wanted the evening to end quickly. The aromas emanating from the restaurant's kitchen were delectable, and Patsy Pritchard wasn't bad to look at, even if she seemed to be wound as tight as a spring.

"Patsy, you must meet my guest," Myrtle Carter said in a tone that reminded Radar of a queen— maybe the silly ruffled collar had something to do with it. "Patsy, this is my new young friend, Sergeant Raymond Darling."

She looked up at him and forced a smile. This

was *so* awkward. She'd seen this man in his skivvies; his well-honed physique had been bared to her, the memory of which made if difficult for Patsy to breathe, much less speak. And he looked military through and through tonight, even dressed casually. That turtleneck stretched tight over a chest that was at least a yard across....

Then he looked down at her and grinned, and Patsy couldn't help grinning back.

Oh Lord, if she hadn't been sitting down, that smile might have melted the hinges in her knees. "Sergeant Darling," she murmured, hoping that her agitation wasn't evident in her voice.

"Please, call me Ray," he said and offered his hand.

Patsy accepted it. "Ray," she said, a slight catch in her voice. Now she'd be given away for sure. Her heart was beating like a tom tom, and she was certain that Sergeant Darling would be able to feel her pulse racing when they shook hands. Or maybe he wouldn't. His grip was so tight that Patsy was sure she wouldn't be able to move her fingers for at least an hour once he let it go.

Patsy jerked her hand away and shook it to get the circulation going again. "At work they call me Pat."

"Sorry," Ray said. "It's easy to forget one's own strength."

"I may not be able to move my hand for days," Patsy said, flexing her fingers.

"Silly," Aunt Myrtle said. "No harm done. Your fingers are working just fine." She turned to Ray and patted the empty chair between Patsy and herself. "Please, sit down. We've been waiting to order."

Ray sat, then picked up his menu and perused it. "What's good here?" he asked, looking over the top of the menu. Just seeing his raised eyebrows set Patsy's heart fluttering.

"Anything and everything," Patsy answered, still slightly breathless. The reason she knew about the menu was that Aunt Myrt often brought her here.

"Then I think I'll try the amberjack," Ray said, closing the menu.

Like the grande dame of the manor, Myrtle signaled for the waiter who scurried right over and took their orders. Then they settled back to wait.

"Why don't the two of you get acquainted while I go powder my nose?" Aunt Myrtle suggested.

That was the last thing she needed, Patsy thought. To be left alone with superhero-in-disguise Sergeant Darling. Even in the middle of this crowded restaurant.

"Sure. But, your lovely niece and I are already old friends," Ray said.

"Oh?" Myrtle, a frown of consternation on her face, stood poised halfway in and out of her chair.

"Yes. I have had occasion to partake of her professional services at the clinic from time to time," Radar said.

At least, he hadn't mentioned the most recent event, Patsy was relieved to hear. How she had hated jabbing that needle into that firm, perfect butt, though looking at it hadn't been a chore at all. She felt her face grow warm. "Yes," she said, nodding vigorously, hoping that the motion would erase the flush. It didn't. "I've seen him in the clinic." Boy, had she seen him!

"Well, that's even better than I'd hoped. You're already friends," Myrtle said, more to herself than them, as she hurried away. She paused to speak to the waiter, then hurried out of the main dining room.

Friends? Patsy thought. I hardly think so. Enemies. Not hardly. Boyfriend/girlfriend? No, she shouldn't be thinking about that. After all, she had a firm policy about dating men she saw at the clinic. Any men, really, but maybe her aunt was right. Maybe it was time for that to change.

"So, your aunt calls you Patsy," Ray said, placing his napkin in his lap and leaving his hands braced against his muscled thighs.

"Yes," she said primly, happy to have been afforded the change in her direction of thinking. She put her hands in her lap as well. "She's the only one I let get away with it."

"Why is that? I like it. It suits you," Ray said.

She'd liked it, too, when her parents had called her that, or her late husband. But it seemed as though everyone who'd ever cared about her had died and left her alone, so she didn't encourage that particular intimacy anymore. It evoked too many memories. "I don't!" she lied, her voice sharp.

"What do you want me to call you, then?"

Patsy knew well what the men in the clinic called her behind her back, so she had to give Ray an alternative. "Pat will be fine."

"All right, Pat," Ray said. "Pleased to meet you." He paused. "Do you come here often?"

Patsy had to smile. It almost sounded like a pickup line. "Yes, it's one of Aunt Myrtle's favorite restaurants. Our family had a summer home on this stretch of beach years ago. I'm afraid Hurricane Opal took care of it, and Aunt Myrtle didn't bother to rebuild." She glanced around the familiar restaurant. "The hurricane took the Blue Heron out, too, but they rose from the rubble." She smiled. "I must admit, I liked the old version better."

Ray glanced around the room, decorated in the traditional trappings of Gulf Coast seafood establishments: old fishing nets, shells, starfish, stuffed fish, or maybe they were fakes, he didn't know. It looked like any or all of at least a hundred other restaurants on the Gulf of Mexico. "Has it changed much?"

Patsy shrugged.

As Ray inspected the room, he paused and glanced out the window that overlooked the parking lot. A moving car caught his eye. "Look, it's a vintage Cadillac, complete with fins. You don't see many of those around anymore."

Patsy jerked her head around so fast to look that she almost dislocated her neck. "Oh, no! That's Aunt Myrtle's car!"

"She must be moving it to a better parking spot."

"I wish," Patsy muttered. *No such luck,* she thought as the waiter arrived with only two salads.

Ray looked up. "You forgot one."

"One what, sir?"

"One of the salads. There are three of us."

"Oh, no, sir. The lady cancelled her order. Said she had a headache. But she told me to tell you to please stay," the waiter assured them. "Miss Carter said there was no reason to ruin your evening."

None, indeed, Patsy thought. "She probably planned this," Patsy muttered, placing her napkin on her plate and pushing herself up. "I should have known." She blew out a frustrated puff of breath as she hurried to the window, her eyes flashing with anger.

Then Ray realized what Miss Carter was up to. She had left him alone—if you could call being left in a crowded restaurant on a Saturday night being alone—with Prickly Pritchard, the ice princess. And he wasn't sure he minded one bit. If Nurse Pat Pritchard was something to see in her starched white uniform at the clinic, she looked even better dressed in casual clothes. The blue eyes that had always appeared so icy and cold seemed warmer now, brighter, almost turquoise. Who would have thought that Prickly Pritchard could ever look that soft and inviting? Even in khakis and a sweater. Ray felt his trousers grow tight, and wishing circumstances were different, he willed himself to behave.

If she looked this good in casual clothes, dressed up, she'd be magnificent.

Patsy scanned the room, looking for someone, anyone, she could ask to take her home.

Ray joined her at the window, and Patsy felt even more trapped than she had before. But pleasantly so, she realized.

"You might as well calm down," he said. "You'll just end up with indigestion."

"That'll be my problem, then, won't it?" Patsy snapped as she peered out the window. She all but pressed her face against the glass, hoping against hope that Aunt Myrt really had just moved the car. No such luck. As if she hadn't known already. The only kind of luck she seemed to have was bad.

Patsy drew in a deep breath and turned, pasting on an artificial smile. No sense in letting gorgeous Ray Darling see her lose her cool. That was certainly not the image she had worked so hard to project at the clinic. "She's gone," Patsy said with forced calm as she hurried back to her seat and primly placed her napkin on her lap.

"I do have my own transportation," Ray said as he seated himself again. "I didn't hitchhike to get here. I know that we special ops guys are known to be rough and tough, but we do draw the line."

"What?" Prickly Patsy shook her head. "What does that have to do with me being stranded here, miles from home?"

"I didn't walk," Radar replied with the type of patience one reserved for five-year-olds—or idiots. "I do have a car."

"A car?" Sheesh, she sounded like a moron. "Of course. Well, I'll just eat my salad and we'll go."

"I think not," Ray said firmly, sounding nothing like the darling sergeant she had begun to think of him as. "Your aunt paid for a full meal. We will eat the entire meal. And we'll enjoy it." He sounded just like a drill instructor.

"Yes, sir," Patsy snapped, then approximated a salute.

Ray chuckled. "At least, you used the right hand." Then he dug in to his salad, and Patsy was glad he was occupied for the time being.

She made a face, and turned her attention to her own salad. "This *is* a little nicer than staying home with my dog, my VCR and black-and-white movies," she murmured, her mouth full. Now why had she volunteered that particular morsel of information?

"You like old movies?" Ray asked, his eyes brightening with interest.

Patsy blushed. Ray had picked right up on her comment. Were they actually trying to make conversation? She swallowed. "Yes. And I hate it when they've been colorized. It makes them look too bright. Too artificial."

"And seeing things in shades of gray isn't?"

Did he want to argue, or was he merely making conversation? Patsy swallowed another bite of salad. "You know what I mean. The colors are often wrong."

"Yes, I understand. Do you just enjoy the classics, or anything not in color?" Ray forked another bit of salad.

"My favorites are *Casablanca, The Treasure of the Sierra Madre* and *The Maltese Falcon*."

"A Humphrey Bogart fan, then," Ray concluded. "What about the Three Stooges or the Marx Brothers?"

"Too silly. No woman likes them. What's funny about three grown men poking each other in the eye and bonking each other on the head?"

"Harold Lloyd?"

"Better. At least, he's not mean-spirited. But I prefer stuff that pretends to have a plot." Patsy swallowed. Had she really said that?

Ray chuckled. He had such a nice smile, Patsy couldn't help noticing. "I have to confess that I like old science fiction movies."

"Attack of the Killer Centipedes, and The Blob that ate Albuquerque? Those kinds?" Patsy suggested, making up names.

"*Planet Nine from Outer Space.* Probably one of the best worst movies ever made." Ray laughed. "And one of my favorites."

Patsy couldn't help smiling. Was Ray actually a fan? "You know Ed Wood?"

"Know him? I love him!" Ray broke into a wide grin. "I probably have every one of his movies memorized."

You would, she couldn't help thinking, but in a nice way. Ray had been reputed to be smarter than the average airman, but she'd never really had a conversation with him until now. What chitchat they'd had always seemed to lean toward the weather or the reason he was at the clinic. Now she was finding out that his interests were different than those of the typical airman, but she'd bet he was into computer games. If not computers themselves.

"I just ordered the complete Wood collection off the Internet," she found herself confessing.

"Oh, man," Ray said. "I think I'm falling in love."

Then the waiter arrived with their food, and Patsy turned gratefully to her Deviled Crab. *Saved by the dinner bell,* she couldn't help thinking as she chewed. Another minute and she might have found herself inviting Ray to her place for an Ed Wood Film Festival.

In spite of her reservations, Patsy was enjoying her "date" with Ray. Of course, she'd never let on to Aunt Myrtle. And deep down she knew that she wasn't ready to invite this man, any man, into her home. She still had secrets she wanted—no needed—to keep.

RAY ORDERED the Pecan Praline Pie just to extend the evening—even if he would have to run a couple of extra miles next week to make up for it. He might be as hard and tough as an armadillo's kneecap, but he had to work at it. His weakness had always been dessert.

At least, Prickly Patsy had ordered dessert as well. Did she always eat dessert or was she, too, looking for a way to keep the evening going?

"I am going to regret this," Patsy said as the waiter placed the Death by Chocolate in front of her. She inhaled the rich aroma. She hadn't even taken a bite, and Ray thought she might swoon. That was certainly a side of Prickly Pritchard he would never have imagined. The guys at the base often wondered if she survived on a diet of pickles and prunes.

"That good, huh?"

"Just the aroma seems sinful," she said, slicing off a piece with the side of her fork. She raised it to her lips, but didn't open her mouth. "Maybe if I just look at it, and only breathe it in, I won't gain twenty pounds." She looked at Ray and grinned. "No, I'll gain it anyway just from being in the same room with it," she said wryly. "I might as well go for the complete experience."

Patsy popped the chocolate confection into her mouth and slowly withdrew the fork. She wore an expression of pure bliss as she chewed, and Ray wondered if that was what she looked like when she made love. What would it feel like to have her underneath him and to give her that much pleasure? Would she respond like...?

He gave himself a mental shake to rid himself of the image in his mind's eye, but he almost exploded as he watched Patsy eat. To keep himself sane, he took a huge bite of his own dessert, and understood why Prickly Pritchard had had such a powerful reaction. The desserts here were too damned good to be legal.

"Oh, man. I think I've died and gone to heaven," he muttered.

"Even if paying for it will be hell," Patsy said. "I'll have to take a couple of extra aerobics classes to pay for this."

"Yeah," Ray said with a groan. "I'll probably have to run ten extra miles."

Patsy laughed and Ray loved seeing it. Here, she seemed so different from the stern, prickly nurse he'd seen so often in the clinic.

"I should think you'd be used to it," she said. "Don't you run wearing forty pound rucksacks on a regular basis?" She leaned on her hand and watched him with an interested expression.

"Not if I can avoid it." Ray patted his stomach. "And after all I've eaten tonight, it might feel like I'm carrying two rucksacks."

"You can handle it," Patsy said. "You have plenty of muscles, from what I've seen." She looked quickly down at her plate, but not too quickly for Ray to notice the flush that colored her alabaster skin with an embarrassed stain.

Was she thinking about the other day in the clinic when she'd had a free look at his rump, or was she embarrassed about making such a personal statement? Ray pushed his plate away and decided to change the subject. "Well, I've had plenty. More than plenty." He signaled for the waiter.

"Sir?"

"We're ready for the check."

"The other lady took care of it," the waiter said. "The one who left."

"I see," Ray said, annoyed that Miss Carter had paid for his meal. He'd fully expected to pay for this evening.

And it didn't make him happy that the evening was about to come to an end. Considering Prickly Pritchard's reputation for turning down dates, this was probably his one and only chance.

The question was: For what?

And why? was another question. The answer to that one was clear: he really liked this Patsy Pritchard. From what he'd learned about her tonight, there was a whole lot more to her than her clinic demeanor suggested. But was his attraction due to the challenge her "at-work" attitude presented, or was it a genuine attraction to the woman he'd glimpsed tonight?

He looked at Patsy again.

All of the above, he decided.

Chapter Three

Though she had enjoyed dinner with Ray once they realized they had interests in common, Patsy didn't look forward to being trapped, alone with him in his car for the thirty-mile trip home. He was too big, too attractive, too real.

And it had been a very long time since she'd been with a real man. Not since Ace. And she knew how that had ended. If it hadn't been for her sending him out that night, he would still be alive today.

"What's the matter, pretty lady?" Ray asked as he escorted her out through the parking lot toward his waiting car.

Patsy jerked her head up to look at him. Had she been so transparent that he could read the mood on her face? She shook her head, more to banish the negative thoughts than to deny her mood. "Just thinking about something. It doesn't matter." Not to Ray, anyway, Patsy thought. To her, it mattered very much. Still. She glanced out at the quiet waters of the Gulf. ''Oh, look at the sparkles on the water!''

Ray turned to follow her gaze and smiled. ''The phosphorescence.''

''I used to think it was magic when I was a little girl,'' Patsy murmured.

''Then you learned that it was a bunch of microorganisms. Were you terribly disappointed?''

''Devastated,'' Patsy admitted. ''It destroyed my belief in fairies and mermaids.'' She hadn't realized it, but they had subconsciously changed their direction and were now heading toward the dark beach.

Ray chuckled. ''I didn't have any illusions to destroy. I'd already learned all about it before I saw it. The waters are too cold to hang around the beach at night in Washington, where I'm from.'' He shrugged. ''I didn't see it the first time until I went to the navy dive school on Key West.''

The sea breeze off the Gulf was chilly. Patsy tugged the two sides of her sweater together, crossed her arms over her chest and tucked her hands into the opposite sleeves. As cold as she was, she really wasn't ready to end this date with Ray. Even if she was still annoyed with Aunt Myrtle for tricking her into it. Even if her aunt's intentions had been good. Even if this ''blind date'' seemed to be working out much better than Aunt Myrtle's setups usually did.

She certainly wasn't about to tell Myrtle that. Patsy smiled to herself. She wouldn't dream of giving her aunt the satisfaction.

"Ah, that's better," Ray said.

Patsy looked at him just as the breeze picked up and blew her hair into her face. "What's better?" She tried to shrug the hair out of her face, but only succeeded in getting it in her mouth, and she was too cold to uncover her fingers and brush it away.

"May I?" Ray asked, nodding toward the recalcitrant lock of hair.

She arched an eyebrow in assent, and Ray gently brushed the wayward strand away. He paused, allowing his fingers to linger on her cheek, and Patsy swallowed, wondering what would come next. Did she actually want him to kiss her?

What if he did?

No, worse than that. What if he didn't?

Ray turned his face into the onshore breeze. To him, it was invigorating, reminiscent of his summers on Vashon Island on Washington's Puget Sound. But, he hadn't failed to notice the chill on Patsy's cheek. As much as he didn't want to end the evening so soon, it was time to get Patsy into the car or she'd be shivering, chilled to the bone.

"I think March is still a little cold for walking

on the beach,'' he said. "This is *north* Florida, after all.'' Ray shrugged out of his jacket and draped it over Patsy's shoulders.

Patsy looked up and flashed him a brilliant smile. "Thank you,'' she said. Had she been shivering? "It didn't seem quite this cold outside when I left Aunt Myrtle's earlier.''

"The shore breeze can blow through you fast. I read somewhere that more people contract hypothermia when temperatures are above freezing because they don't think they can and aren't prepared.''

Ray touched Patsy's waist and was surprised at how small she felt beneath his hands. But, then most women seemed small to him. Every woman except one: his mother. Even if she was only five feet nothing, she'd always seemed huge to him.

His mother. The last time he'd seen her or his father, he had just turned eighteen. That night he had left home, against his parents' wishes, to enlist in the air force....

Patsy stumbled in the loose, shifting sand, and Ray automatically reached out to catch her. She looked up at him, and the expression in her face seemed expectant, questioning.

Ray wanted to reach down and tip Patsy's chin up. He wanted to kiss her the way the guys did in all the movies, but he was Ray Darling, boy genius and adult nerd. He didn't have the moves.

The night had been going so well up until this point. He wasn't about to jinx it now. It would kill him if Patsy turned away. He caught her arm and any hint of the windy chill left him as welcome warmth suffused his blood.

"I… Ah… Thank you," Patsy said, and Ray had to stifle a chuckle. Was that the proper etiquette for the situation?

"For catching me," Patsy clarified.

"Any time," he said flippantly. He wouldn't have minded if she had kissed him by way of thanks, but she hadn't, so Ray guessed the moment was gone. He sighed. Maybe if he'd had a normal childhood, he might know a thing or two about what to do at times like this.

"Something wrong?" Patsy asked.

"Not really. Just having some regrets." Then realizing what he'd said, he stopped and looked down into Patsy's lovely blue eyes. "Not about tonight. Not about you," he said, his voice coming out huskier than he'd intended. He tried to figure out how to explain his family situation.

He shrugged. "When I got to thinking about summer in Washington, it reminded me of my parents."

"Are they no longer living?" Patsy's eyes always contained a look of sadness that seemed to deepen now. Ray wondered if she'd suffered some kind of a loss.

"No, they're fine and healthy. At least, I think so. They're just not speaking to me. For nearly ten years now."

Patsy arched an eyebrow. "Why?"

"It's not important." Ray turned and trudged on. "We had different ideas about what I should do with my future," he said, shrugging.

Patsy stopped him with a hand on his arm. "Family is important to me. I'd give anything to have my parents back."

"They're gone?"

"When I was in grammar school," Patsy said softly, lowering her gaze downward toward the damp sand. "Aunt Myrtle raised me after they died in a plane crash."

"I'm sorry." What else could he say?

Patsy looked up at him again and flashed him a brilliant smile that seemed to light up the dark. "About what? That Aunt Myrtle raised me?"

"No," Ray started to say, but then he saw that the quip was Patsy's way of shifting from an unpleasant subject, so he dropped it. "I bet it was fun living with Myrtle."

"It was," Patsy said. "But it wasn't quite normal. We lived in a big old house by the water, and

I never felt comfortable inviting my friends over. We always had to be so careful, with all her antiques and objets d'art all around. And Myrtle was reluctant to let me do some of the things that I wanted to do, so I often rebelled.'' She paused. ''And I always wanted brothers and sisters.''

''Me, too.''

''You're a lonely only?''

''Well, I was always too busy to be lonely, but yeah, I'm an only child. Let's just leave it at that.''

They'd reached the parking lot, and there didn't seem to be anything left to say. Ray was content to listen to the night sounds as they trod on the crushed shells in the parking lot. The crunch of the shells, the wind as it whispered through the scrubby trees and the tinny sound of the jukebox from the Blue Heron all combined to create a unique symphony. And even if he never got another chance to go out with Prickly Patsy Pritchard, he knew he would never forget this night....

AT LEAST HE DIDN'T HAVE one of those teensy sports cars, Patsy thought with relief as Ray ushered her toward his compact recreation vehicle. The single guys at Hurlburt Field were divided into two groups: the ones who bought sports cars, and the ones who were into trucks and SUVs. Radar didn't seem to fit into either category. Was that a good thing? She thought perhaps it was.

And he got points for opening the door for her, too. A CRV was a lot smaller than a truck or a sport utility vehicle, she realized once she was in the passenger seat and Ray had carefully shut the door. The two of them would be in close quarters in the front seat. Would he try to kiss her now that they were so close?

Patsy felt her heart rate increase, and she suddenly felt warm. Of course, she was still wearing Ray's coat. It felt so good around her shoulders, almost like a hug. She could smell the fragrance of his aftershave and the manly scent that was uniquely him on the fabric, but reluctantly, she shrugged the jacket off.

"Be sure to buckle up," Ray said, and Patsy complied, happy to have something to do for the moment. Then he closed the door, and the vehicle got even smaller.

Or was it just her?

How long had it been since she'd sat alone in a car with a man?

She couldn't remember when. Once the kids were born, she and Ace had never seemed to be alone.

"Would you like to listen to the stereo, or would

you prefer to talk?'' Ray asked as he inserted the key into the ignition.

''Music, I think,'' Patsy said, then wondered if Ray would interpret that as a rejection. ''I'm curious to see what kind you like. Not techno-metal, I hope,'' she said, forcing a smile.

Ray made a face, and Patsy hoped it wasn't because he did like that kind of music. ''I'll let you decide for yourself,'' he said, turning the key. He let the car idle while he selected a CD from a case he'd stashed in the console.

He inserted the disk, and the soft strains of Carole King filled the air. Patsy hummed along as she listened. The selection surprised her, but then she thought, it shouldn't have. Every time she'd come to a conclusion about Ray Darling, he'd countered it with something new. And she rather liked the surprises.

As they waited to turn onto Highway 98, the next song came on. Definitely not Carole King. Then she recognized it: Garth Brooks's alter ego, Chris Gaines. She liked that song, too.

''I mix and burn my own CDs,'' Ray explained as he accelerated along the dark highway.

''So, I guess that means you're pretty good with computers, then.''

Ray grinned. ''Love 'em. I'm the squadron expert, even if we actually do have techies on staff.'' He chuckled. ''That's part of the reason they call me Radar.''

''Oh, then it's not for Ray Darling?''

''No,'' Ray said emphatically. ''When I first got assigned to the squadron, I got a lot of ribbing because of my name. You don't know how many times I got called just plain Darling.''

There was not one thing plain about him, Patsy thought. Not even when he wore glasses.

She smiled. ''Oh, I can hear it now. I need to speak to you, dar-ling,'' she said in a saccharine sweet tone. ''Hand me that wrench, dar-ling.''

''Exactly. I had to come up with something that would distract the guys from my name. So I dazzled them with my computer skills.''

''I'm impressed,'' Patsy said. ''I can use the programs we have at the clinic, and I can word process and do e-mail, but that's the extent of my computer literacy.''

''Well, some of those old guys, the ones close to retiring were really resistant when I first came in. You know, they were used to doing it one way, and they didn't want to try anything new.'' He chuckled. ''I talked 'em into it real quick. Chief Mullins was the one who started calling me Radar. I think radar was one of the few technical things he was familiar with. It saved my butt. I was tired of getting into fights about being called darling.''

"I'm sure you could have handled them," Patsy said. "You don't look like you'd lose many fights."

Ray smiled wryly in acknowledgment. "Unfortunately, my technical expertise didn't do much for my airman proficiency ratings when they were countered by reports of those fights," Ray said, frowning. "I think it kept me as a staff sergeant for an extra cycle, in spite of my test scores."

Patsy had wondered why he hadn't made technical sergeant yet. He certainly seemed worthy of the promotion.

"But I made it this round," Ray continued. "I'm waiting to see when my number comes up. Don't know whether I'll make tech first or get selected for Officer Training School."

Patsy arched an eyebrow, surprised to realize that somehow he'd managed to snag a college degree, a requirement for all OTS candidates. "You graduated from college? Was it the adult education college on the base?"

"No," Radar answered sharply. "The University of Washington," he clarified. Then he seemed to set his jaw as if he wanted no further conversation.

Okay, Patsy thought. If that was it, that was it. She settled back against the seat and listened to the music. Something from James Taylor this time.

RAY HADN'T HEARD anything from Patsy's side of the car for a while, not that he could blame her for being quiet. He had been damned short with her. And for no good reason. At least, not one that she'd readily understand. How do you explain that you graduated from college at seventeen and then joined the air force to find out what it was like to be a real guy?

Hell, she might turn on him for wasting his education just as his parents had.

Why couldn't anybody understand that the air force had been an education, too? And that he still had plenty of time to go on to graduate school. And when he did go, he'd be a lot better prepared for it than when he was a kid.

He glanced in Patsy's direction. No wonder she'd been so quiet. She seemed to be sleeping.

Though he needed to keep his eyes on the road, he kept glancing Patsy's way. She looked almost like a child with her arm resting against the passenger-side armrest and the hard glass window pillowing her head. So serene, so relaxed. So very kissable. Radar chuckled quietly to himself. He wondered if he'd ever get the chance.

No, not if. When.

Ray smiled to himself. Prickly Pritchard was sleeping with him. Okay, maybe not in the biblical sense, but it still struck him as funny. Every single guy at Hurlburt Field had been speculating about who would be the lucky guy to get through Prickly

Patsy's reserve, and he had. Too bad he couldn't tell anybody.

Of course, he'd never kiss and tell. Not that they'd kissed yet, nor was there a guarantee that they ever would. And if he did, he doubted anybody would even believe him. Not Radar Darling, the sergeant most likely to…break his glasses.

He hummed along with the music and steered the car through the strip of tourist motels and across the Okaloosa Bridge, which took them into downtown Fort Walton Beach. He supposed he'd have to wake Patsy up now. Otherwise, he wouldn't know where to take her.

He stopped at a red light, and nudged Patsy's shoulder. He'd like to kiss her awake, but that wouldn't work in the confines of the car. And it was presuming a lot more than he dared at this point in their relationship. Assuming it wasn't an end.

Patsy jerked awake, obviously startled.

"I didn't mean to frighten you," Ray said. "We're back in town. I need to know where to take you."

Patsy blinked, vaguely trying to register where she was and what she was doing in this car with Radar Darling. The red light blinked to green, and the car surged forward while Patsy struggled to clear her muddy thoughts.

"Make a right on Beal," she said groggily, then stifled a yawn. "Then a left on Hollywood."

"Roger that," Radar said, executing the first turn.

"I apologize for nodding off on you," Patsy said, stifling a yawn. "I was up late last night."

"Did you work an extra shift at the hospital or something?"

Patsy had to laugh. "No, the job at the clinic is enough work. I just stayed up too late watching an old movie on television. I'm afraid it's one of my worst weaknesses. Then I got up early to take Tripod to the vet."

"Tripod?"

"My dog."

Ray nodded. He'd always wanted a dog. His parents had said it would be a distraction from his studies.

"Is he sick?"

"She. No, she was just getting a rabies booster."

"Tripod is not exactly the kind of name I'd associate with a female dog," Ray said, turning onto Hollywood Boulevard.

"You'd have to meet her. Then you'd understand." Patsy looked up. "Oh, sorry, I wasn't paying attention and let you drive past the turn. Turn around and then take the next right. I live in the third duplex on the right."

Ray made the turn a little sharper than he would have preferred, but then the inertia caused Patsy to lean against him as he made the turn. He smiled as he turned onto her street, then counted the houses, small cinder block bungalows with carports on either end. "Which side?"

"I've got the one on the left," Patsy said. "You can pull up behind my car in the carport."

Ray did so, then halted the car and turned off the engine. He wondered if he should try for a kiss now, or wait until they got to the door, but Patsy took the decision out of his hands. She pushed open the passenger door and scampered out.

Ray had to scramble to catch up with her. "Where I come from, we walk our ladies to their doors."

"Thank you," Patsy said primly, "But this is a perfectly safe neighborhood. I'm not in danger of being mugged. And I'm not *your* lady."

"Touché." Ray grabbed at his chest as though she'd been a fencer and had nicked him with her epee. That was the Prickly Pritchard he'd come to know and love, Ray thought, relishing the idea of trying to get through to her again.

Patsy slowed and let him catch up with her as she walked to the door to the house. At the sound of her footsteps, a dog inside the house began barking excitedly. At least the barking sounded fairly friendly, Ray thought.

"What are my chances of getting to meet your roommate?" he asked. "I won't sleep until I know why you call her Tripod."

Patsy laughed, and the icy pall lifted. "I would hate to be responsible for keeping you up all night," she said as she fished in her bag for keys. Ray hoped that meant that he'd be invited in. "Tripod was close to dead when I found her," Patsy explained.

"So you rescued her and nursed her back to health," Ray concluded.

"Not quite. I took her to the vet, thinking he'd put her to sleep, but he said that he could save her. Most of her, anyway."

"Most of her?"

"He couldn't save her left foreleg, so she limps," Patsy said, smiling fondly as she leaned against the doorjamb.

Ray grinned. "Got it. Three feet—Tripod." He had to admire the woman. Not everyone would take in a three-legged dog. "I like that," he said.

Patsy looked up at him, real confusion on her face, and Ray wanted so much to kiss her. He reached toward her, but she ducked away. "You like what?" she asked.

"That you took pity on a poor, injured dog."

"Oh," she said. "I guess I'll go in now." She offered her hand. "Thank you for driving me home," she said as though she were reciting something she'd learned in etiquette class.

"You're welcome," Ray said, accepting her hand and feeling the warmth and silky texture of her skin against his. He rubbed his thumb over the smooth skin on her palm. "I was kinda wondering what my chances were of getting invited in to watch the Ed Wood Film Festival."

"Not tonight," Patsy said, sounding nervous.

Ray grinned. "That wasn't exactly the answer I was looking for, but it does give me hope."

Patsy looked surprised. "It does?"

"Sure. Not tonight implies that another night might be in our future." He smiled down at her, hoping she'd pick up on the hint.

"We have no future," Patsy snapped.

"We all have a future, Patsy," Ray said gently.

Instead of arguing with him as he'd expected, Patsy's eyes clouded up, and before he knew it, she had jerked open the door, darted inside and slammed the door behind her, leaving Ray standing there with the finality of that last gesture echoing louder than the sound of the door. "Just what the hell was that all about?" he muttered to himself.

Then he heard the bolt turning in the lock.

PATSY STOOD INSIDE the house, her back pressed firmly against the door, Tripod jumping up against her in greeting, her tail wagging wildly. Normally, she loved the way her dog said hello, but tonight she was not in the mood. She reached down to pet the dog, but her heart wasn't really in it.

Why had Ray gone and spoiled it all?

For the first time in years, she'd gone out with a man and had actually begun to enjoy herself, and he'd ruined it for her. She'd even thought she might be ready for a good-night kiss, but Ray had gone and reminded her of everything she hadn't been able to forget with that remark about the future. Of course, she had a future, and Radar had a future, but there had been no future for Ace and her children, and that was her fault.

Tears welled in her eyes, and she tried to blink them back. Loving and caring for people was wonderful, but losing them was almost like dying herself.

It seemed as though everyone she'd ever cared about had died. Now, rather than running the risk of being hurt again, she found it easier to just not care.

That was why she didn't date. That was why she could never see Ray Darling again. She might come to care for him. Losing anyone else would just hurt too much.

Tears spilled from her eyes and ran down her cheeks, scalding her skin, and rubbing salt into old wounds that never quite seemed to heal.

RAY STOOD IN THE DIM LIGHT of Patsy's carport and tried to figure out what had just happened. He'd thought that everything was going pretty well. Prickly Pritchard might not have completely melted in his arms, but he had thought he'd detected a definite thawing.

He drew in a deep breath, shrugged and turned toward his car. She might not have allowed him a good-night kiss, but there was still that Ed Wood Film Festival to look forward to. She *would* agree to the evening.

It just wouldn't be tomorrow.

Or next week, but soon.

He'd bide his time, and when the time was right, they'd watch those movies together. And next time it wouldn't be because an old lady with good intentions had paid for them to be together.

Next time, it would be because they both *wanted* to be together.

Chapter Four

Patsy tried to forget the date with Sergeant Darling, but thoughts of Ray would not leave her alone. For weeks.

The memory of that evening, and the kiss that should have happened, just would not let her be. She found herself in those half-awake moments just before she fell asleep imagining that kiss. And then, she'd dream.

In the light of day, she tried to convince herself that she was being silly. After all, she was twenty-seven years old, widowed and had lost two children. She wasn't exactly a giddy teenager with dreams of a happily ever after.

Still, she found herself hoping that Ray Darling would come into the clinic. She watched for him at the base snack bar at lunch and looked for his face atop every uniform she saw outside. She was never rewarded by as much as a glimpse of him.

Ray Darling seemed to have disappeared from the face of the earth or, at least, from Hurlburt Field. And for all practical purposes, her life.

Then on one particularly hectic April afternoon when she had more things to do than she had time or hands for, one of the doctors directed her to splint and bandage a badly sprained ankle he'd already examined.

Patsy bustled into the examination room with the materials she needed and nearly stopped in her tracks. There on the table, wearing gray coaches' shorts and a T-shirt, was the object of her daydreams. The sprained ankle she was there to attend to belonged to none other than Sergeant Ray Darling. Funny, with all her watching, she hadn't even seen him come in.

For some reason, she didn't know what to say. She just looked at him as if she wasn't sure she was really seeing him.

"A hello would be nice," Ray said, easing back on his elbows against the exam table and gazing lazily up at her. In spite of the discomfort he was obviously in, he flashed her a grin, and that made Patsy suddenly feel all hot and bothered.

"Hi," she said, the pitch of her voice a little too high to sound casual. "When Doctor Brantley said there was a sprained ankle in this room, I didn't know it was yours.'' She knew it sounded pretty stupid, but it was the truth.

''Well, right now I'd give this ankle to anybody who wants it,'' Ray said, grimacing as he shifted. ''Free!''

Ray's apparent discomfort and his admission finally caused Patsy's nurse training to click back in. ''I'm sorry,'' she said. ''The sooner I get it immobilized, the sooner it will begin to heal.'' She forced herself to stop looking at Ray's face and to concentrate on the red and swollen joint. ''You're going to have to stay off it for a while, you know,'' she said as she began to quickly and efficiently wrap his ankle.

''Won't break my heart, considering how it feels at this moment. I sure hate to let the team down, though,'' Ray said, punctuating his statement with a sharp intake of breath when Patsy jostled him as she made the final turn with the elastic bandage. ''Hey, that's a real leg in there!''

Patsy pressed the binding hooks into place and smiled. ''Sorry. I thought pain was nothing to you combat-control types.'' She handed him a pair of crutches. ''Do you know how to use these?''

''I think I can figure it out,'' Ray said wryly, positioning them beneath his arms. ''For the record, we don't usually admit we're in pain, but we damn sure feel it.''

"Oh, just wanted a little sympathy, then?" Patsy said, sitting down at the computer in the corner of the office and making some notes in his medical records. "You're on light duty for at least a week," she said. "It's official. I don't want to hear about any twenty-mile hikes in full gear." She turned to Ray. "How did you do this, anyway?"

Ray managed a sheepish grin. "I was demonstrating the proper way to slide into base," he said, indicating a streak of dried dirt on the left side of his shorts and some red scrapes on his thigh. "I caught my foot on the d— Excuse me. The stupid base and this was the result," he said indicating the injured ankle. "Graceful, huh?"

"Well, your team will have to do without you for a couple of weeks. Keep the foot elevated for a day or two, and stay off it!" She turned and consulted the computer. "The doctor put in a scrip for a painkiller. I suggest you use it."

"I don't need no stinkin' painkiller," Ray growled, affecting a tough-guy tone. "Just give me a bullet to bite."

Patsy rolled her ryes. "Take it home with you, at least. You know, if the bullet doesn't work, the pills will be there. They will ease the inflammation and will actually help your ankle heal faster."

"All right," Ray said. "Under one condition."

"I hardly think you're in a position to bargain

with me right now, Sergeant," Patsy said, her hands on her hips in a parody of the intractable nurse character the men saw her as. "I can tell the doctor you're being uncooperative, and he can confine you to quarters."

"I surrender!" Ray said, propping himself on the crutches and raising his hands in a white-flag gesture. "I was just going to invite you to watch the team play some afternoon if you have time."

"I don't know," Patsy said. "I stay pretty busy here until after six."

"Not on Saturdays," Ray pointed out.

"True," Patsy had to concede.

"Then it's a date. You come watch the team next Saturday. I promise, I'll be on the bench." Ray grinned at her. "We're out on the field behind the Youth Activities Building. We start at three. First game of the season. You can be our good luck charm."

Not hardly, Patsy thought, but she'd go. Not because she was that interested in a bunch of grown men behaving like children, but to be certain that Ray kept his promise about staying off his foot. At least, that was what she told herself. "All right. I'll see you there."

"Saturday afternoon. Three o'clock." Patsy wasn't sure what she was getting into, but she convinced herself she was going to make sure that Ray didn't reinjure himself.

Ray flashed her a little-boy grin that made Patsy feel all soft and mushy inside. Then he maneuvered himself out the door to collect his prescription from the pharmacy. Even on crutches and in pain, the man looked too good to ignore.

THE DAY WAS BRIGHT, the sky clear with only a few cotton ball clouds dotting the blue expanse. With a slight breeze, it was a perfect day for a baseball game. Only Patsy's arrival would make it better, Ray thought.

He squinted in the bright sun, training his gaze away from the playing field and in the direction of the parking lot. Still nursing his tender ankle and propped up on his crutches, Ray watched to see if Patsy would really show up. He wasn't at all confident. He was still making up for lost time regarding the man/woman thing.

The team was busy warming up, and there was still time for her to show up before the game started at three, but not much. It would have indicated a modicum of interest on her part. Ray hated the idea that it might be a mercy date.

Not that it was really a date.

Somebody tugged at his shirttail and Ray looked

down to see his third-baseman. "Mr. Radar, Bwian keeps frowing the ball too hard."

Davey, the tail-tugger, was the youngest boy on the team, just barely too old for tee ball, but not really ready to hold his own with the bigger boys. His big brown eyes welled with tears. "I can hit the ball, sir. I weally can."

"All right, my man, we'll just have to see about that," Ray said, reluctantly tearing his gaze away from the parking area. "You go over there and I'll toss you some balls. You show me what you can do."

Dragging the heavy wooden bat that was almost too big behind him, Davey trudged a few feet away. He parked his sturdy little body into batting stance and lifted the bat into position. Ray pulled a ball from one of his pockets and tossed one right at the bat. It hit the wooden club with a dull thud and bounced a couple of times, then rolled a few feet farther. You would have thought that Davey had hit a home run, though. The boy grinned a gap-toothed grin as Ray scooped up the ball.

"I knew you could do it, buddy," Ray said, reaching out and tousling the boy's thick brown hair. "Let's try another one. Do you think you can step back a little farther this time?"

Davey stepped back and Ray tossed another one at him, this time not aiming quite so precisely at the bat. Davey swung and, to his apparent amazement, hit the ball with a resounding crack. It popped up high and Ray caught it with his bare left hand.

"Good shot, my man. Let's do one more, then it'll be time to start lining up to play." He'd seen the other team gathering around their bench on the other side of home base. "Step back."

Davey did and Ray threw. Again the boy hit the ball, this time sending it flying out into the field.

"Another good one. I knew you could do it." He lifted his hand in a high five, then dipped it low so Davey could reach it. Still the boy had to jump up so his little hand could meet Ray's, and Ray grinned. "Better go round up the ball and get ready to line up," he said, then Davey scurried away.

Someone behind him began to clap. "Good show, Radar," Patsy Pritchard said. "Why didn't you tell me you were coaching a peewee team?"

Ray spun around, nearly losing his balance on the crutches. It hadn't occurred to him that Patsy would think otherwise. "Would it have made a difference?"

Patsy shrugged. "Probably not." She glanced to where Davey had finally caught up with the ball. "That was a nice thing you did there," she said.

"What? Tossing a ball with my guys? It's part of the job."

"Not that. Building the boy's confidence like that. I saw the way you eased him into it."

"Just as long as Davey didn't."

A dog yipped and Ray looked down to see a three-legged animal on a bright pink leash prancing around trying to get his mistress's attention. "The world-famous Tripod?" he asked.

"The one and only," Patsy confirmed as Ray reached down and allowed the dog to lick his open hand. "She wasn't thrilled about being ignored."

"Pleased to meet you, Miss Tripod," Ray said, and Tripod wagged her stubby tail so hard the action threatened to knock her off balance.

"She likes you," Patsy said, approvingly.

"Obviously she's a very discerning canine," Ray said, looking up into Patsy's big blue eyes. She always looked great in her uniform at the clinic, and she'd looked equally good in the khakis and sweater she'd worn to the restaurant, but in white shorts, a peach halter top and a floppy, straw hat, she looked better than fantastic.

Patsy laughed. "Tripod likes everybody. It's a good thing I had her fixed. She's just a little too easy."

"Ouch. You wound me," Radar said, pretending to clutch at his heart.

"You'll live." She glanced over his shoulder at

the sound of a whistle. "Uh, oh. It looks like they're ready to start."

Ray glanced back and saw that the other team was getting into position. "Well, gotta go." Ray signaled for the guys to line up by their bench, then turned back to Patsy. "Will you and Tripod be here when we're done?"

"We'll be here."

Ray turned and maneuvered himself toward the group of boys and grinned triumphantly. She had shown up. Patsy Pritchard had really come! Apparently, Prickly Pritchard wasn't nearly as starchy as she pretended to be. She liked three-legged dogs and children. She might not want anybody to know it, but she was a real softy inside.

He liked that.

He liked it a lot.

FLIPPING UP HER sunglasses and shading her eyes with her hands, Patsy watched as a player from the other team hit a pop fly. The game had been tied until this point, but that one hit could change the score. As she watched the boy scamper to first base, making it possible for another hitter to get a turn at bat, she wondered how little Davey would take losing the first game.

Funny, she thought as she watched the final moments of the game, she'd always steered away from events involving children. And truth be told, if she'd known this was a kids' game, she wouldn't have come. She'd feared that being around children would dredge up feelings and emotions that had taken her years to suppress. Yet, sitting here in these splintery, wooden bleachers, all she felt was joy.

These boys were having the time of their lives. And so was Ray, if the grin that hadn't left his face was any indication. He was loving every minute of the game, even if he had to love it on crutches. Patsy was glad that she hadn't known that Ray was coaching a boys' team. She would have hated to miss this. If she hadn't come, she wouldn't have seen this other side of Ray Darling.

The crack of yet another ball being struck pulled her attention back to the game. Little Davey, stationed way out in left field, caught the ball, much to his amazement, and the game ended. The other team had won, but to Davey it wouldn't matter. Just catching the ball that put the final batter out and ended the game was enough to make him feel like a hero for the day.

She jumped up and cheered just as loudly as the rest of the spectators. Even Tripod joined in, barking happily along with the joyful noise.

Finally the tumult settled down.

She was glad she'd been there to see it. And she hadn't even known the boy before today.

"Are you up for pizza and sodas with us?"

She'd been so busy watching the grinning boy run to his parents that Patsy hadn't noticed Ray come up behind her.

"I'm sorry. Did you ask me something?"

"Wanna join us for pizza?" He crooked his arm like he expected her to take it. "My treat."

"Oh, yes. You've made an offer I can't possibly refuse," Patsy said, tightening her hold on Tripod's leash, and taking Ray's arm. She enjoyed the delightful tingling sensation that just touching him brought her. "Will Tripod be able to come?"

"The restaurant has a patio, so I'm sure our friend will be welcome," Ray said, dropping one crutch and bending down to pet the dancing, tail-wagging dog.

"Works for us," Patsy said. "Your car or mine?"

"Come with us. I'll bring you back to the car after we eat," he said as he scooped up his crutch.

"Us?"

"Gotta take a couple of kids with me. Not everybody's parents could make it here for the game. You don't mind, do you?"

"Not as long as the kids don't. You know how boys that age feel about...*G-I-R-L-S!*" Patsy said, spelling the word, then made an appropriately disgusted face.

Radar shrugged. "They'll deal with it. Besides, pizza with the guys is a pretty good incentive for a kid to put up with a girl—cooties or no."

"I guess. Never having been a boy, I wouldn't know." All she did know was that Sergeant Ray Darling was a very nice man, and the more she got to know about him, the more she wanted to know him.

"Trust me. I was. Pizza is a great incentive to get a guy to do anything. At any age," he added as they strolled toward his vehicle, two sweaty, grubby boys cavorting as only boys could as they hurried ahead of them.

Patsy smiled. "Just one thing," she said as they reached the familiar little CRV. "Don't let it out that Prickly Pritchard likes little boys."

Ray stopped, apparently startled, and balanced on his crutches. "You know about that?"

"The Prickly Pritchard thing? Of course. It doesn't bother me." In fact, she'd done everything she could to cultivate the nickname. "Just don't let on. Please?" The last thing she needed was to suddenly have people thinking she was a soft touch.

"Sure," Ray said. "Loose lips sink ships."

"Whatever. Now, let's hurry up and get to that

pizza. I'm sure those kids are starving. And Tripod could probably do justice to a couple slices.''

"You sure it isn't you who's hungry?'' Ray challenged.

"I'll never tell,'' Patsy said. And she'd never tell anyone that she was sincerely glad that Aunt Myrtle had fixed her up with Ray Darling. She certainly wouldn't admit it to her aunt, but maybe it really was time that she started living again.

RAY SAT ON THE HARD cement picnic bench outside the Pizza Palace and watched the way Patsy interacted with the kids. If anyone was a natural, she was. He wondered why she wasn't married with a bunch of kids of her own.

But then, if she were married, he wouldn't be sitting here.

"What happened to Tripod's leg?'' Brian asked as he slipped another piece of pepperoni to the dog.

"She got hit by a car when she was a puppy and her bones were broken too badly to fix,'' Patsy told him matter-of-factly. Ray liked the way she hadn't tried to dodge the question, and she hadn't given the kid more information than he really needed to know.

"Oh. She sure gets around good, though,'' the kid said, then turned back to carefully plucking pieces of mushroom off the remnants of his slice of pizza.

"If you're still hungry, we could order another one," Patsy offered, watching the way the boy devoured his food.

"No, ma'am. I'm all full up." He looked up and grinned delightedly. "Look, there's my mom!"

Ray turned to see Brian's mom, dressed in rumpled BDUs, get out of her car. Her tired face lit up and she smiled when she saw her son. She waved and double-timed it over to them.

"I'm so sorry I missed your game, Brian. How'd you do?" She squeezed him to her.

"Aw, Mom. I'm not a baby anymore," Brian protested, pushing away from her embrace. "We were tied 'til the last minute, but the other guys won."

"But they put on a great game," Patsy interjected.

"I'm sure you did. Are you ready to go?" his mother said, her gaze sliding toward the pizza.

"Yeah." Brain shoved the last of his slice into his mouth, gathered his cap and glove and hopped off the bench. "I'm ready."

"Thanks for waiting with him. With Brian's dad deployed, there don't seem to be enough hours in the day," the woman said.

"Any time," Ray said.

"We've got a couple pieces of pie left, if you're hungry," Patsy volunteered, and her stock went up another couple of notches in Ray's esteem. It was obvious that Brian's mom was tired and hungry, and not having to go home and fix her own dinner would probably be greatly appreciated.

"Thanks," she said. "I'd love some."

Patsy wrapped the slices up in a couple of napkins and passed them across the table to the tired woman. "Have a good night," she said.

And Ray was pretty sure she would. He watched the woman trudge tiredly to her car, Brian scampering along beside her, talking animatedly to her, telling her about the game. Ray turned to Patsy. "That was nice."

"What? Giving her the leftovers?"

"Well, yeah. I didn't think about it." And he wondered why he hadn't. He well knew what it was like to spend a full day out in the field and then to have to come home and scrounge for something to eat. Until recently, he'd lived in the dorms and could go to the chow hall, but now that he'd moved off base and was sharing an apartment with Danny Murphey, one of them had to cook. Or they both went hungry. A sergeant's pay could only afford a limited number of meals out.

"I was just saving myself from them," Patsy said flippantly. "I'm sure I ate enough this afternoon to make my clothes too snug for the rest of the week.''

"No, you didn't. You made sure the kids were fed, the puppy was fed and then you made sure Brian's mom was fed. Don't you ever think about yourself?''

Patsy shrugged. "Sure. About once a week, I have a nice long, soak in the bath.''

"Oh, yeah. I bet that recharges your batteries,'' Ray said, his tone heavy with irony. But just the thought of Patsy naked, surrounded with fragrant bubbles, was enough to have his shorts feeling a little snug. He reached for the pitcher on the table and poured himself another glass of ice-cold soda. He knew cold showers were supposed to work; but he didn't know whether the cold drink would achieve the same result. All he could do was hope.

Just then, Davey and his parents—also eating at the pizza place, came over and stopped in front of him, and Ray's interest in Patsy wilted. At least, the physical evidence of it did.

"You guys off?'' Ray asked Davey.

"Yes, sir,'' Davey said. "I sure had a good time today.''

"Yes, he did,'' the boy's mom interjected. "And we did, too. I don't know how much we can thank you for what you did.''

"And what would that be?''

"You know."

Ray did know. He'd just hoped it hadn't been that obvious. It was enough to know that Davey had felt like a big man in spite of the team's loss.

"Davey's always the youngest, no matter what. His birthday falls in January, so though he's old enough to do things according to the rules, sometimes it doesn't work out in practice."

Ray well knew how that felt. "One day, all that won't matter anymore," he said. "All we have to do is help him get through it now as painlessly as we can."

"Well, you're doing a great job."

"I'm doing the best I can."

Patsy punched him on the arm as Davey and his parents walked toward their car. "Stop with that *aw shucks, ma'am* bit," she said. "You did a good thing. Why don't you just accept the thanks gracefully?"

"I don't know." Ray shrugged. "I guess I'm just not used to compliments." When Ray had been growing up, nothing had ever been good enough. His own parents, well-meaning as they might have been, had never seemed satisfied. They had always wanted him to do more, to try harder. Being a smart kid had come with a lot of pressure. He sure wouldn't inflict that on any kid of his.

If he ever had kids.

No, *when* he had kids.

He'd have kids, and he would not do any of the things to them that his parents had done to him. He didn't want them trying to make up for lost childhoods when they were adults, as he was doing now.

PATSY WATCHED THE SHADOWS flit across Ray's face. What could have him thinking so hard? "Penny for your thoughts?" she asked, holding her hand out, a penny on her palm.

"Huh?" Ray looked up at her and seemed to shake himself out of his thoughts.

"What has you in such deep thought?" She closed her hand over the penny and put it away.

"Nothing. Just thinking about how hard it's going to be for Davey until he catches up."

"Davey's a trooper. He'll catch up in no time, especially when he has somebody like you watching out for him."

"I hope so," Ray said. "Being younger than your peer group isn't always easy, and those few months can make a big difference at that age."

"Sounds as though you've had experience with that."

"You could say that. I was always the youngest kid in my class. It can do things to the way you think about yourself."

"Why?" Patsy said, as she began to gather up the stuff from the picnic table.

"It's hard to explain," Ray said. "It just does."

Patsy stuffed the trash into a can, and looked at Ray. "Now what, coach?"

"Time to go, I guess," Ray said, still looking pensive as he gathered up his crutches.

"So soon?"

Ray rewarded that remark with a smile. "Yes, ma'am. If you look, you'll see that all the kids have gone."

"Why, I do believe you're right. It's just you and me and the pooch." Patsy tightened her grip on the pink leash. "Come on, Tripod. It's time to go home."

Tripod wagged her stubby tail, and Ray had to laugh as he maneuvered himself onto his crutches. "All right. Let's head back to the car."

Patsy couldn't help thinking that she wished it were really a date, but then she did have the dog, and she'd have to get her home and feed her something other than pepperoni scraps for dinner. Maybe it was time to invite Ray over for that Ed Wood Film Festival. As much as she'd been eager to watch the films, she hadn't been able to make herself sit down with them since that blind date almost a month before.

Because of Ray's crutches, Pasty let herself into the car and waited for Ray to seat himself. Once he did, he turned to her and said, "Do you think Tripod would mind if I kissed her mistress?"

Chapter Five

Patsy's breath caught. It was broad daylight, cars were all around them in the parking lot and people were coming and going. "I—I don't know what to say," she stammered.

Tripod seemed to be wagging her tail in assent. The little darling, Patsy couldn't help thinking. Maybe now *was* the right time.

"Then don't say anything," Ray said as he leaned toward her.

Wisely, Patsy didn't.

With the dog's tail wagging in approval, she just tipped her head up and waited for Ray to kiss her.

Ray wasted no time in accepting her unspoken invitation.

He kissed her, tentatively at first, then he deepened the kiss. It had been so long since Patsy had felt a man's hard form against hers, felt the rasp of his beard against her tender skin, that it was as though she were waking from a long sleep. She might have tried to forget it, but once experienced again, it was as addictive as a drug.

She had to have more.

Now.

Patsy moaned softly and parted her lips in an invitation that Ray quickly accepted. His heart beat a sensual rhythm against Patsy's breast as he explored and Patsy savored. She wished they were anywhere but in that tiny car with a canine chaperone.

Reluctantly, Ray broke the kiss.

Patsy drew back, a half smile playing on her well-kissed lips. "It's been a long time," she said by way of explanation, her voice weak and quavering. Her hand trembled as she placed it over her heart. "Thank you."

Ray grinned. "Any time," he said.

A car horn sounded, and Patsy wondered if the passengers in that car had witnessed the entire spectacle. Was it a toot of approval or were they reminding them where they were?

Ray turned the key in the ignition. "I guess we'd best get going," he said as the engine caught.

"Yes, probably so," Patsy agreed, her voice still sounding slightly breathless.

Tripod yipped to get her two-cents' worth in.

"All right, puppy," Patsy said. "We're going

home.'' She glanced toward Ray who put the car into gear and backed out of the lot.

''You're welcome to come to any of our games,'' Ray said as he drove. ''Same time, same place, every week till school's out.''

The dog barked as if she'd noticed that she'd been left out of the invitation.

''And Tripod is welcome, too.''

''We'll take it under advisement,'' Patsy said.

She moistened her lips, and she swallowed. ''You know, I still haven't watched those Ed Wood films,'' she whispered, uncertain as to how he'd respond.

''Oh?''

''Maybe we could get together to watch them some time,'' Patsy suggested.

Ray looked as though he wanted to cheer. ''Name the time and place and I'll be there,'' Ray said. ''I'll bring the popcorn.''

''I'll check my calendar,'' she said. ''And then I'll get back to you.''

The ride back to the playing field was much too short and far too soon they were back at the lot.

''Well, this is it,'' Ray said, reaching to undo his seat belt.

''No, Ray,'' Patsy said, touching his arm. ''I can let myself out. You're still incapacitated.'' She leaned over and pecked him quickly on his cheek.

Quickly, so she wouldn't lose her nerve. Then she let herself out the door, Tripod hopping gamely down behind her.

"Thank you. I enjoyed it," Patsy said, looking into the open door. Then she closed it.

Ray seemed to wait a little too long before he started up the car. Patsy wondered if he wanted to say something else, do something else. But he didn't make a move. After a long moment, he backed away.

Patsy watched from her own car as Ray drove away. She looked down at Tripod. "Well, girl," she said. "I wonder just what I've gotten myself into."

Tripod just wagged her tail.

IT WAS ALL RAY COULD DO to keep from rolling down the window and shouting, "Hoo-ah," at the top of his lungs for all to hear. But he was damned certain she would not like it if he kissed and told. What would he do about Danny, he wondered. His roommate would be able to tell something was up simply from the expression on his face. He'd have to think of something. Seeing Danny had been so out of sorts since going on his own mystery date after the bachelor auction, Ray knew it would be far better not to gloat, anyway.

He shrugged and steered his car toward the base

gym. Maybe a good upper body workout would help him wind down.

He was thrilled that Patsy had liked him well enough to accept another invitation, and to issue one—albeit a vague one—of her own. Not to mention that she had let him kiss her—and had kissed him back. And if he wasn't mistaken, she'd enjoyed it as much as he had.

"SERGEANT DARLING?" Patsy called, her voice breathless, in spite of herself. She tried avoiding searching the waiting area for his handsome face and held the thick medical folder against her white-clad chest as if it were a shield.

She hated being so formal, but there was no way she'd loosen up here in public at the clinic. She still had a reputation to uphold.

She just hoped Ray would remember that.

Ray, clad in his regulation battle dress uniform, pushed himself up to his feet with his crutches and maneuvered himself to where she stood. "Yes, ma'am," he said.

"This way." Patsy struggled to keep her tone businesslike. "Examination room three."

As soon as they were alone, she allowed her expression to soften. "Are you ready to throw those things away?" she asked, indicating the crutches.

Ray shot her a grin that could have lit up the darkest night. "Am I? Do you even need to ask?"

Patsy smiled and shook her head. "I didn't think so. The doctor will check you out, but I'm pretty sure you'll be relieved of them."

"Hoo-ah!" Ray cheered, and Patsy grinned. "Free at last."

"I have to commend you for sticking with them as long as you have. Most of your teammates would probably have tossed them out and been well into physical training by now—doing permanent damage to themselves, I might add," she said sternly.

Ray laughed. "You don't know how tempting that was, but I didn't want to get on your bad side."

"Miss Pritchard, stop flirting with the sergeant and let's get the man cleared for normal duty again," Dr. Brantley said, stepping into the examination room.

Patsy felt her cheeks grow warm, and Ray grinned. It hadn't occurred to her that she'd been flirting, but that was exactly what she'd been doing, she supposed. She was so out of practice, she hadn't recognized her actions for what they were. She stepped back and watched as the doctor did his job.

"Keep your workouts light for a few days," the doctor said, slapping Ray on the shoulder. "Then you can get back to your regular routine."

"I hear that!" Ray said. He reached for the

crutches and handed them to Patsy. "I don't suppose they'd let me burn them, so here," he said, thrusting them in her direction. "Do with them what you will."

"We'll recycle them," Patsy said. "I'm sure one of you gung-ho guys will need them within the week."

"Whatever," Ray said, shrugging and testing his weight on his injured ankle. When it seemed to hold him, he laced up his jungle boot and tried it again. Then he stood, unaided on both feet, and glanced at Patsy, a questioning look in his eyes.

Something about his expression made Patsy go soft and gooey inside, but she waited to hear what he had to say. She didn't want to jump to conclusions.

The doctor left the room, and they were alone.

"You had a question, Sergeant?" Patsy said, keeping her tone neutral in case anyone else came by.

Ray glanced out the open door into the corridor. "Yes, about that film festival…?" he asked, leaving an opening Patsy didn't hesitate to fill.

"Saturday night. My place," Patsy answered in a rush. She forced herself to slow down. "I'm expecting you to bring the popcorn."

"I will be there with alacrity," he said.

Patsy laughed. "Not alacrity," she corrected.

"Popcorn. You can't watch Ed Wood without plenty of popcorn."

"Wouldn't have it any other way," Ray said, with that endearing grin that made Patsy wish it weren't still so early in the week.

She watched Ray, favoring his ankle only slightly, stride out of the room. She was so glad he wasn't leaving permanently.

She'd done it.

She'd actually asked Ray Darling out on a date. A surge of warmth and well-being flooded through her and she smiled to herself.

Ray stopped and glanced over his shoulder. "One question," he said.

Patsy arched an eyebrow, and wondered whether the question was of a medical or personal nature. "Okay?"

"Do loose lips still sink ships?" he asked, referring their discussion of the weekend before.

Patsy wished she could say no, but she still felt awkward about this dating thing. Maybe later on, she'd feel more confident, but for now, she wanted to keep her relationship with Ray quiet. She sighed apologetically. "For now, yes," she said.

"Got it," Ray said, then he hurried out, and Patsy wished he didn't have to go.

RAY STOOD IN the commissary in front of the popcorn display and wondered what he'd gotten himself into. Who would've thought that there were so many kinds to choose from? Had there always been that many choices? He pushed his glasses up on his nose and perused the shelves again. Or had he just not paid attention?

He finally settled on a brand he remembered being advertised on television and started to reach for the package. But wait—there were other things to consider. Microwave, hot-air popped or regular? Damn, this was confusing.

He grabbed a couple of packages of each type and hurried to the register line. Of course, it was Saturday afternoon and the line wasn't short.

At the rate he was going, he might get out of there in time to get home and get cleaned up. He glanced at his watch. Or he might not.

Finally, the line inched along and he reached the register and paid for his selections. And he'd thought that bringing the popcorn would be a simple matter. He hoisted his sack into his arms and walked out just as he saw Sergeant Rich Larsen and his pretty wife and baby come in. He waved, and much to his chagrin, Rich headed his way while his wife secured the baby into the shopping cart.

The last thing he needed was to have to explain to Rich Larsen why he was buying the entire stock of the popcorn section. He'd promised Patsy he would not tell, and tell he would not.

At least, not until Patsy felt better about it.

"Shopping for the bachelor pit?" Larsen asked.

Ray shook his head. "Naw, just stocking up on snacks to watch some movies by."

Rich shook his head. "Yeah, I used to do that. It sure is better when you have somebody to watch them with," he said, indicating his pretty wife and child. "Maybe you should get out more."

"Maybe I should," Ray agreed.

"You do that." Larsen glanced over his shoulder and turned back to Ray. "See ya, Radar. Jennifer's got the cart ready to go. I guess duty calls."

"See ya," Ray said, and breathing a figurative sigh of relief, he headed out of the store.

As he drove, he began to think about the secrecy of this date with Patsy. The more he thought about it, the more he began to wonder why she was so dead set against anyone knowing that she was dating him. Did it have something to do with him?

And they *were* dating. Even she would have to admit that. The last time they were together might not have counted as a date—until they'd kissed. Then everything had changed.

Once she'd actually invited him to her home, they were dating. Whether anyone else knew about it or not.

One thing was sure, Ray thought as he parked in

the lot outside his apartment, he was going to get
to the bottom of it. He was going to find out just
why Patsy Pritchard didn't want anybody to know
about them.

TRIPOD STARTED UP a merry round of barking, and
Patsy parted the blinds to see what had gotten the
dog going. She should have known. Ray Darling
had just pulled into the drive and parked his CRV
behind her car.

"Shush, Tripod. It's just Radar," Patsy said as
she made a quick pass by the mirror on the wall by
the entryway and checked her makeup and hair. She
was as ready as she'd ever be.

Now, she just had to let Ray in. It seemed like
hours passed before he came to the front door. And
it would not do for her to rush to the door and open
it before he got there.

Finally, the expected knock came, and Patsy took
a deep breath, wiped her damp hands on her skirt
and pasted a smile on her face. She opened the
door. "Right on time," she said, for lack of anything else to say.

"That's me, always-on-time Darling." He
paused as he said that so that it almost sounded as
if he'd called her darling, but Patsy knew what he
meant. Still, she liked the way that sounded.

"Well, come in, come in. Before Tripod escapes."

Ray stepped inside and bent to pet the excited dog. "You wouldn't run out on me, would you, girl?"

Tripod yipped as if to agree with him. Once the door was closed, she seemed to lose interest and wandered off. That was just fine with Patsy.

"What do you have there?" she asked, indicating the sack Ray was carrying.

"I said I'd bring the popcorn," Ray reminded her.

Patsy laughed. "But you didn't need to bring enough to feed the entire population of Fort Walton Beach. There are only two of us. Three, if you count Tripod, and she doesn't eat that much." She reached for the bag. "Here, let me take that from you."

Ray handed it over. "Who would've thought there were so many kinds to chose from? I just sort of bought a selection."

"That you did," Patsy said wryly as she glanced into the bag. "I don't know where to start. Do you have a preference?"

Ray sank down onto the sofa and looked around the homey living room. "If I had a preference, do you think I'd have bought so many different kinds?"

"I don't know. Would you have?" Patsy called from the kitchen. He heard the sound of something being opened and, after a moment, the sound of an appliance coming on. "What do you want to drink?"

"I don't much care," Ray said and wondered why he hadn't thought about that before now. What if she had some strange taste in beverages? Should he have brought some beer or a six-pack of soda? "Whatever you're having," he called and hoped it wouldn't be diet soda.

She came in after a moment with glasses and ice and a couple of cans of soda. She also had two long-necked bottles of beer. "Take your pick."

Ray took a beer, and Patsy nodded in approval. "We can have the sodas later." The microwave dinged and Patsy turned to retrieve the popcorn.

"This won't last long," Patsy commented as she placed the bowl on the coffee table. "I put another one in so it would be ready when we were."

"Good thinking," Ray said. Would they ever get past all this ridiculous small talk? He definitely wished he could have found and memorized an instruction manual for this dating thing.

He'd been out with a few women since he'd been in the air force, but most of them had been friends first. And none of them had seen his butt before-hand—not that many had seen it after. No, before

Patsy Pritchard, it had never seemed as awkward and uncomfortable as this.

Was all that discomfort a good thing? A sign of nervousness due to attraction? Or did it mean that he and Patsy weren't going to click?

Patsy settled down on the couch beside him and reached for the remote control. "Ready to get going?" she asked.

"Sure thing," Ray said, casually maneuvering his arm to rest on the back of the sofa, only inches away from Patsy's shoulders. "Let's get this affair started."

And he wasn't sure he meant the film festival.

THOUGH SHE'D SEEN the movie before, Patsy found herself laughing so hard that tears ran down her cheeks. How could anyone have taken these things seriously? she wondered as she wiped tears from her eyes. "Ouch!"

Ray stopped in midchuckle and paused the video with the remote control. "What's the matter? Did you hurt yourself?"

"Silly me," Patsy replied. "I forgot there was salt on my hands from the popcorn and when I rubbed my eyes, I got it in them. It stings, but it'll be okay."

Patsy's eyes burned and teared, and the one eye that had gotten the bulk of the salt had slammed shut. Patsy could see the concern on Ray's face with the eye that hadn't been as badly affected.

"Here, let me look at it," Ray said, taking her face in his two large hands. He gently pried her burning eye open and looked closely. "I guess that is one advantage to wearing glasses. You have sort of a barrier to keep irritants out."

"I suppose," Patsy said. It felt strange to have someone looking at her, holding her in such an intimate way, though there was nothing sexual in Ray's tender ministrations. But it had been so long since Patsy had experienced anyone worrying about her, trying to take care of her, that his doing so touched her. If she weren't already tearing up because of the salt, she would have done so now with emotion. The tears continued to flow.

"That's it," Ray said. "Just let them wash the salt out."

"You'd think that since tears are already salty, it wouldn't hurt that buch," Patsy said, her nose stuffy as a reaction to the tears.

"Tears are saline, but the salinity is nothing compared to full-strength salt," Ray said, voicing something that Patsy already knew from her nursing training. She'd been joking when she'd made that crack. "Do you have any eyewash?"

"Id the bathrube, I thik," Patsy said.

"I'll get it." Ray started to leave, but turned and kissed Patsy on the nose first.

Now she was really in trouble, Patsy thought. Who could resist a knight in shining glasses coming to her rescue? How wonderful it was to have someone to care for her, care about her!

How she had missed being pampered and spoiled. Even though she and Ace had been poor as church mice, they'd always managed to do things for each other. She missed that, but surprisingly, the thought didn't cause the horrible aching pain that remembering her late husband had always done before.

She smiled to herself. Maybe she really was finally healing.

"Feeling better?"

Patsy looked up to see Ray returning with a bottle of saline eye drops in his hand. He knelt in front of her. "Let me put these in."

Patsy leaned forward and allowed Ray to administer the drops. They seemed to ease the discomfort almost immediately. "Thank you," Patsy murmured. "That feels so much better."

"You know, you're not the only one with medical training here," Ray said, pushing himself up and easing back onto the couch. "I'm certified in first aid. I just never get a chance to use it," he said. ''I wonder if I'll ever get to show my stuff,'' he said, almost wistfully.

It was the wrong thing to say. For the past few weeks, Patsy had managed to convince herself that it didn't matter that Ray was in an occupation that could put him in harm's way at any moment. Now, he seemed almost too eager to get his chance to play war.

There was currently a situation in the Middle East that didn't seem to want to settle down. Patsy knew that Ray would have to take his turn there sooner or later, and she sensed he wouldn't be at all unhappy about going. That was one of the things she hated about the airmen that she ministered to. They were all too eager to get into the fight.

She stiffened and pulled away. ''Don't say that,'' she said a little too sharply. ''There is nothing glorious about death and dying. And if you think there is, then maybe we should quit right now.''

Ray backed up against the back of the couch and held his hands up in a gesture of surrender. ''Whoa, hold it. I didn't mean anything by that.''

''Yes, you did,'' Patsy snapped. ''Just like every one of you gung-ho guys, you want to get into the middle of the fighting. Don't pretend you don't.''

Ray drew in a deep breath. Patsy was probably right. He did want to put his training to use. He hadn't trained and practiced for the past ten years only to sit and watch footage on the evening news. He knew that war was hell, but still he wanted to feel useful. He just didn't know how to explain it to Patsy.

"Patsy," he said carefully, taking her small hands into his. "I don't want to throw myself in front of an oncoming tank. I have special skills that I'd like to get to use. Did you know that I'm a trained weather observer?"

Patsy's eyes widened, and she shook her head.

"They used our guys in Afghanistan to get weather reports to Central Command. I wasn't there, but some of the guys from here at Hurlburt were. They had to drop in behind enemy lines to do the job, and they were prepared to fight if they had to, but they didn't want to."

He looked off into space. "I studied meteorology in school. It's something that fascinates me. I'd love to be able to use what I know."

"I thought you were referring to your emergency medical training," Patsy said, flexing her fingers still enclosed in Ray's hands.

"Sure, I'd like to use it. I'd like to feel useful." Hell, he'd like to prove to his parents that he hadn't wasted his education by running away to enlist, but he wouldn't go into that now.

"And I'd like to be able to get to an accident scene and save somebody's life," Patsy said, and

Ray wondered if there was more to that statement than just the words. "But, I spend my days giving shots and wrapping ankles. It doesn't mean that I'm wasting my training."

"Yeah," Ray said. "You're probably right." He glanced toward the image frozen on the television screen. "Do you want to see the rest of the movie?"

Patsy nodded, and Ray pressed the play button on the remote.

He didn't pay much attention to the rest of the video. After all, he'd seen the movie more than once. He focused his mind on his odd conversation with Patsy. He might actually have gotten a little insight to what made her tick, Ray realized. She was afraid to get involved with military guys because she feared losing them.

That wasn't such an unusual fear, but it seemed to go far deeper than that with Patsy. It seemed personal. Now, he just had to figure out why that was.

FEELING LIKE A TEENAGER on her first date, Patsy held open the front door for Ray. He started down the walk, and Patsy's hopes fell. He wasn't going to kiss her. Maybe her outburst had pushed him away. She turned back into the house, her eyes filling with unexpected tears.

If she'd run him out of her life, then why did she want to cry?

"Patsy?"

She turned, her eyes full of unshed tears. "Yes? Did you want to take the rest of your popcorn with you?"

"No," he said, striding back to her. "Save it for the next installment of our film festival."

"What, then?"

"This…"

Chapter Six

Ray took her by the shoulders and pulled her to him. "I've been wanting to do this all evening," he whispered as he lowered his face toward Patsy's and kicked the door shut.

Their lips met, and any thought of tears fled from Patsy's mind. All she could think about was the strong man holding her, the way he smelled and tasted, with just a hint of beer and salty popcorn on his lips. The slight rasp of his beard tantalized her as his face brushed against hers and evoked a mental image of warm bodies on cool sheets. Theirs. How long had it been since she'd thought of anything like that?

Eager to feel his heart beating against hers, Patsy wrapped her arms around him and drew him yet closer. She felt, rather than heard, him sigh, and she smiled inwardly. How had she managed to go on for so long without this?

A tiny, but unsettling, thought kept surfacing even in the midst of so much pleasure. How would it feel to lose something like this again?

She started to push him away, but Ray pulled her back, and Patsy didn't resist. The joy of what she was feeling was too strong. A little moan of pleasure escaped from her. Maybe she could learn to live for the day and not worry about what might be.

Then Tripod started to nip against her shoes.

Saved by the dog. Darn it.

Shaken and trembling with desire, Patsy stepped out of Ray's arms. "I wonder if it's possible to train a dog to use a litter box?" she muttered as she glared down at the dog.

Tripod sat on her haunches and cocked her head as if to say, "I'm cute, and you know it."

"I hear it's been done, but I imagine it isn't an easy process." He looked down at the adorable pup at their feet. "Who can turn down a face like that?" Ray said, his voice husky.

The dog pranced back into the living room and returned, dragging her leash.

"Smart dog," Ray said. "I know her timing is bad, but maybe it's better this way. There's nothing wrong with slowing this down. We have plenty of time."

"Yes, I suppose," Patsy said, not trying to conceal her disappointment. She reached down to connect the leash. Did they really have time? she wondered.

"Next week?"

"Same time, same place," Patsy said, straightening.

Ray leaned in and pecked her on the cheek, and Patsy couldn't help wishing that she'd gotten more of him, more of his delicious kisses earlier. But time and Tripod waited for no man.

She opened the door and Tripod dashed out, yanking her forward. Ray followed her out and closed the door behind him.

As the dog sniffed around in the St. Augustine grass on the dark, dewy lawn, Ray climbed into his car. Patsy raised her hand to wave, and Ray waved back.

This wasn't goodbye, she reminded herself. It was "See you later." With that thought, she smiled.

They had plenty of time.

And they'd made a date for next weekend....

MAYBE TRIPOD HAD interrupted them at the wrong moment, Ray thought as he drove himself back to the apartment he and Danny shared, but that wasn't necessarily so bad. There was nothing wrong with taking things slow. There was a lot to be said for the experience of anticipation.

Ray liked the fact that he had next Saturday to look forward to. He liked that there were still some things about Patsy remaining for him to learn. And maybe one day he'd tell her about himself.

He pulled into the lot and his headlights illuminated Danny's car in the next spot. Damn, that meant his roommate had spent another night moping at home. Ray didn't know what had happened on Danny's bachelor auction date, but the man had been hell to live with since he'd come home the morning after.

And Danny had been as close-mouthed about what had gone on that night as he'd been surly. Ray was certainly happy that his date had turned out so much better than Danny's apparently had.

At the front door he prepared himself to face Danny's mood again. He opened the door, and he wasn't surprised.

''You're getting to be a regular man about town,'' Danny said, his voice slurred. ''Used to be, you were the one at home in front of the tube when I came in.'' He was holding a bottled beer with one crooked finger as he sat in front of the blaring television. Some sci-fi movie, which Ray approved of, but it still bothered him that Danny hadn't gone out.

He just couldn't seem to pull himself out of his funk. If the man would just talk about what happened, it might help.

"Nothing keeping you from going out yourself," Ray said lightly, hoping he wouldn't start a fight. His roommate's red-headed temper had been simmering too close to the surface in past weeks, and it didn't take much to make it boil over.

"Not me," he said. Seeming not to take offense. "I swore off women. Don't even want to see one."

"You can go out without seeing a woman," Ray pointed out reasonably.

"What would be the point?" He took a swig of his beer. "I can drink at home, and not have to worry about running into anybody of the opposite sex."

Ray figured that midnight was not the best time to try to talk Danny out of his mood, so he just shrugged and headed for his bedroom. At least, one of their bachelor auction dates had turned out well.

PATSY HADN'T BEEN surprised to learn that Ray was a science fiction fan, but he'd obviously been pleased to learn that she was, too. In fact, they'd finally graduated from home film festivals, to the real thing. She smiled as she drew in the popcorn-scented air in the deserted movie theater lobby.

They were taking in a late-night showing of a current science fiction flick at the local multiscreen theater, and Ray was at the concession stand loading up on popcorn, sodas and movie candy. It was a guilty pleasure, and Patsy was loving every minute of it. She knew it bothered Ray that she still didn't want to make their relationship public, but maybe going to this movie was a step in the right direction.

And if she happened to bump into somebody they knew, she certainly wouldn't duck around a corner.

Ray returned from the snack counter, arms filled with all the good stuff. "Ready?"

"Am I ever," Patsy enthused. "I love the smell of popcorn at the theater."

They hurried through the lobby and found their way to the appropriate auditorium. As they found their seats in the dimly lit theater, Ray waved at somebody. "I just saw one of the guys on the squad," he commented as he settled into his seat.

Patsy turned to see who it was, but the theater went dark and the previews began to play. "Who was it?" Patsy knew most of the men in Ray's squadron, by sight, at least.

"Runt Hagarty," Ray said. "He was alone. I don't think he ever takes his wife anywhere."

"Oh," Patsy said. "One of those guys. He thinks the little woman should stay at home, barefoot and pregnant." She didn't place the name, but then, many of the men in the special operations squadrons had nicknames that she didn't know. Wasn't Ray Darling called Radar by his teammates?

"Something like that," Ray said. "He's not my favorite person, but he's a good combat controller."

"Well, let's not think about him. I'd much rather concentrate on the movie." The coming attractions ended, the movie started, and Patsy dismissed any thought of Ray's teammate from her mind.

RAY SLAMMED HIS locker door shut, tossed a towel over his sore and sweating shoulder, and strode into the shower room. The physical training session had felt good after several weeks of favoring his injured ankle. Some of the other men had grumbled about the killer workout, but he'd relished the opportunity to stretch out his tight muscles.

He turned on the water, letting it stream over his head, allowed his thoughts to turn to Patsy Pritchard. He hated the fact that she didn't want to be seen out in public with him, but her reasons intrigued him. And one of these days, he was going to find out what they were.

Not now, however. He much preferred to think

about Patsy in another context—in a context having to do with hot sex. Of course, that was yet to happen, but a guy could dream, couldn't he? He felt his groin tighten, but he clamped down on his muscles to squelch any outward evidence. It would not do in a room full of naked men.

Runt Hagarty made himself at home under the shower head next to him. "I sure envy you, man."

Ray pretended he didn't hear him, but with Hagarty, subtleties didn't often work.

And they didn't work this time. "Wouldn't mind getting a taste of that Popsicle myself," Hagarty volunteered again as he made a quick pass at his armpits with the soap, then stepped out from under the spray.

"What Popsicle?" Ray said, though he was pretty sure he knew who Hagarty meant.

"You know that chunk of ice from the clinic."

Clenching his own soap so tightly he would probably leave finger marks on it, Ray did his best to ignore the man. He hoped Hagarty would get out of his line of sight before saying anything else to make him even madder. He sure didn't want to jeopardize his promotion at this late date.

"What say we get a pool going to see how long it takes you to get Prickly Pritchard in the sack?"

That was it! Ray had done everything he could

to ignore the annoying little man and what he'd insinuated, but that was just too much. He balled up his fist, reared back and hit the man so hard he went sprawling on the wet tile floor. The only thing that saved the boor from being badly hurt was that Hagarty was wet and slippery, and Ray hadn't been able to get enough purchase to do any real damage.

"What the hell did you do that for?" Hagarty said, rubbing a red spot on his jaw.

Ray turned the water to cold and stepped under the stinging spray. "I don't think I'm going to tell you," he said between clenched teeth. "Because I'd just love to get another excuse to do it again."

Hagarty picked himself up and grabbed his towel from a hook on the wall. Muttering to himself, he hurried into the locker room to dress.

"No doubt, the sonofabitch had it coming," said Rico Scanlon, the new non-commissioned officer from the open doorway. "But I don't think Captain Thibodeaux would take too kindly to you beating up on his best demolitions man every time he opens his sorry mouth." He unwrapped his towel from his waist and hung it on the hook next to Ray's. "I will admit I enjoyed seeing that, though."

"The guy's a jerk," Ray muttered as he twisted the tap shut.

"Can't argue with you on that one," Scanlon agreed. "Just keep it out of the squadron."

Ray wrapped his towel around his middle and headed out into the locker room. Ray generally preferred to settle his arguments with words and not fists, but in this case, he'd been eager to make an exception. However, since Master Sergeant Scanlon had warned him about Hagarty, he'd have to comply.

"Is that a hint of makeup I see?"

Patsy looked up from the notations she was making and frowned slightly. She'd hoped it wouldn't be that noticeable. After a long period of trying not to draw attention to her looks, she'd finally started experimenting with a little blusher and mascara.

Maybe she shouldn't have tried it at the clinic. After all, how often did Ray Darling come in here?

"Is it too much?" she found herself asking Nancy.

"No, it's great. I like it." Nancy returned to her work and Patsy hoped that would be the end of it, but the pregnant woman turned back to her. "All right," she said, "I can't stand it. Who's it for?"

Patsy swallowed. Should she tell or not? It had been so long since Patsy had confided anything to anybody that she was very out of practice, and

Nancy was the closest thing to a best friend she had. "Nobody in particular," she finally fudged. "I just thought I might give it a try."

Apparently, Nancy would have none of it. "Yeah, and I'm going to win the title of 'Miss Swimsuit Model of the Year,'" she said, a knowing look in her eyes. "Don't tell me. I'll figure it out." Then, chuckling to herself, Nancy turned back to the reception desk.

At least Nancy hadn't pressed, and maybe one of these days, she would confide in the other woman. After all, Patsy was so very new to the whole dating thing. When she had last dated, she'd been a love-sick teenager. Her upbringing had been so traditional that she'd had to elope with Ace in order to succumb to her sexual desires. The rules were different now, she supposed. But she still didn't quite know what those rules were.

She might have been a married woman with children a very long time ago, but that had all changed when Ace and the children died. She had lived the past six years more like a cloistered nun than an experienced woman.

Now, she wanted to be with Ray Darling in every way, and she didn't have the slightest idea how to express her desire to him without her telling him how she felt outright. Ray's kisses at the ends of their dates were heaven, but she was beginning to wonder about the next step. Patsy sighed.

She *would* have to talk to Nancy. Just not right now. She wasn't quite ready.

Yet.

PATSY AND TRIPOD had become such regular fixtures at the afternoon baseball practices that Ray and the boys had begun to think of Tripod as their unofficial mascot. Ray loved that Patsy had taken the time to learn all the kids' names and that she cheered them on with the same enthusiasm as their parents. It was a tough job being an air force kid, and Patsy was helping to make it a little easier.

"Run, Davey, run. You can do it," Patsy cheered from her seat on the grass near the practice field.

Davey seemed to glom onto her voice and picked his little feet up faster and managed to slide into third base before the ball. "Hoo-ah!" Ray cheered. "You did good, my man," he called to Davey.

Davey beamed as if he'd single-handedly won the final game of the World Series, and Ray couldn't help feeling as proud as Davey. Lord, he wished he'd been allowed to experience something like that when he was a kid.

But that was then, and this was now. He'd gotten over his childhood of books and studying and tests, and now he was making up for lost time. He couldn't go back, and when he glanced at Patsy lounging so comfortably there on the sidelines, he was pretty sure he didn't want to.

The afternoon sun was sinking lower in the sky, casting long shadows across the playing field. Ray squinted into the distance as he noticed the long line of cars clogging the road that wound around the end of the runway. It was quitting time. If the kids hadn't been making so much noise he might have heard the sound of retreat being played as the flag at the headquarters building was retired for the night.

"Okay, guys," he said, making his voice businesslike and serious. "It's quitting time. Tomorrow's the big game. The Tigers are undefeated right now, but we're going to change that, aren't we?"

"Yeah," the boys shouted in unison.

"What're we gonna do?" Ray challenged.

"Beat the Tigers!"

"Go team," Patsy cheered. "You can do it."

Tripod even barked her own version of a peppy cheer, and Ray hurried over to pet the dog. He'd love to kiss her mistress, but a practice field in front of a group of preteen boys was not the place or time.

He'd have to settle for wet doggie kisses from

Tripod instead of the real thing. "Are we on for later?"

"Aunt Myrtle is expecting me for a 'command performance' tonight," Patsy said, making a face.

"I'm glad it's you and not me," Ray said. He liked Myrtle Carter, but until Patsy was ready to make their relationship public he wasn't about to give the elderly woman any ideas.

"I just hate it that we won't be able to get together tonight," Patsy said, sighing.

"Me, too," Ray said. "But we've got tomorrow night. I want to see that new Merchant and Ivory film. But, if Aunt Myrtle lets you loose early, give me a call on my cell phone. I've got a new computer game I want to try out, but I'll drop that like a hot potato if you call."

"Don't put yourself out," Patsy said, grinning. She started to fold up her picnic blanket, but turned back to Ray. "Wish me luck. You know Aunt Myrtle is going to give me the third degree," she said.

"About what?"

"My love life. You know. Getting married. Having a happily ever after," she replied. "I haven't told her we're going out yet. I don't want to give her the satisfaction. If she knew, I'd never hear the end of it. Gloating is not becoming on a woman her age."

Ray held his hands up in surrender. "She's your aunt. I guess you know best how to deal with her." He grinned. "Let me know when you're ready to release us from the closet."

Patsy punched him lightly on the arm. Then she laughed, picked up her picnic blanket and bag, looped Tripod's leash around her wrist and waggled her fingers in a goodbye gesture.

"See ya," Ray said.

"I'll call you," she said, then hurried with Tripod to her car.

"Emergency?" Aunt Myrtle asked when Patsy's cell phone rang after dinner.

"We'll see." Patsy smiled and reached for the phone. No matter how hard she tried to explain the nature of her job at the clinic, Aunt Myrtle always preferred to think that Patsy was so much more indispensable than she really was.

"Hi. This is Patsy."

It was Ray. Patsy covered the mouthpiece with one hand, turned to Aunt Myrtle, bussed her on the cheek, then said goodbye. "Gotta go, Aunt Myrt. Thanks for dinner. It was great, but it looks like I'm needed."

As soon as she got out of the house, she spoke back into the phone. "You're where?" Apparently,

Ray was baby-sitting for friends. She listened while he gave her directions, and worried about the panic in his voice. Ray always seemed so in control. But the baby crying lustily in the background sounded anything but under control. Ray hadn't given her details; he'd said only that he needed her. Desperately.

She'd hoped he would say those words one day in quite a different context. Still, she was curious, and it was an excuse to break away from Aunt Myrtle a little sooner than she would have been unable to do otherwise. Patsy climbed into her compact car and drove to the address that Ray had given her.

RAY WATCHED FOR PATSY'S car and answered the door in a complete panic. He was totally out of his element, and at this point, didn't care who knew it.

Rich and Jennifer Larsen had promised that Sara would sleep the whole time they were gone, and all he'd have to do was make sure the house didn't burn down. At the moment, he'd have preferred a fire to this squalling baby. He knew how to deal with that kind of emergency. Nothing in his training as a combat controller had prepared him for this.

His glasses were askew, and he didn't have a free hand to straighten them. He fumbled to open the door while he balanced the fretful baby in his other arm. As long as he jiggled the unhappy, little bundle of joy she only whimpered, but the instant he stopped, she wailed at the top of her lungs.

"Thank God you're here," he said as he closed the door behind Patsy. He had never been so glad to see her as at that moment, and he was usually pretty darn happy to see her. He'd stopped jiggling momentarily and Sara took the opportunity to scream at the top of her lungs. Who knew a baby girl had such lung power?

"What's wrong?" Patsy asked as soon as she was inside.

Ray jiggled the bundle in his arms, and the volume of Sara's cries lowered a couple of decibels. "Sara woke up screaming at the top of her lungs and I can't get her to settle down," he said, handing the squalling baby over to Patsy, who seemed unexpectedly startled as he thrust the baby into her arms. For a moment, he thought she might not take her.

Patsy's breath caught and her heart skipped a beat. She wanted to flee as an irrational sensation of panic reared in her chest, but she couldn't run. Ray needed her. No, this baby needed her. She'd have to push her doubts and insecurities aside and deal with them later. She drew in a deep breath and swallowed. Hard. Anything to force the panic away.

Sara seemed startled by the change, stopped wailing for a second or two, then resumed.

Patsy jiggled and the volume went down. "Whose baby is this and why are you with her?" she asked as she felt the baby's padded bottom. "Not wet," she said before Ray could answer.

"She's Rich and Jennifer Larsen's. You know Rich. He's one of the guys in the combat control squadron. I don't usually sit for babies, but their sitter canceled at the last minute and they had tickets for some show that's in town only one night. Jennifer promised that she'd sleep right through, but the minute they were out of sight, she started to scream." He looked at the baby worriedly.

"It's all right, Sara," Patsy crooned. She felt inside the baby's mouth and an expression of recognition came on to her face. "I think she's teething. See how she drools and keeps sticking her little fist in her mouth?"

"I noticed that the front of her shirt was wet and she was slobbery," Ray said. "But aren't all babies? What do we do about it?"

"Show me to her room," Patsy said, adjusting to the familiar feel of a baby in her arms as Sara gnawed on her finger. "There's probably some kind of teething ointment there, and something to chew on."

Ray led the way through the neat little bungalow to the baby's room. Sure enough, there on the dresser was a tube of teething ointment. Funny, he hadn't noticed it before, but then, he probably wouldn't have known what it was for if he had.

Patsy reached for it, still jiggling the baby with one arm, and opened the tube. She squeezed a small amount out on one finger and worked her way into the baby's mouth. Sara seemed to quiet almost instantly. "See, nothing to it," Patsy said.

"Now you tell me," Ray said sourly. "They could have warned me."

"I doubt they expected it," Patsy said, wiping at the drool on Sara's red face.

"But they had the ointment," Ray protested.

"Ever hear of the Girl Scout motto 'Be prepared'?" Patsy countered as she laid the baby back into her crib. "Boy Scout, too, I suppose." Sara fussed a little, but settled down a moment later.

"Never was a Boy Scout," Ray muttered.

"Most babies start to teethe around six months, and Sara's about that age. Her mom and dad were probably anticipating it. It was just rotten luck that it happened tonight."

"I'll say. I would not have come over if I'd even dreamed that the kid would be awake. I have absolutely zero experience with babies."

"That is plain to see," Patsy said, as she motioned for him to come out of the room.

Ray followed her out. "Well, you didn't have to agree with me," he grumbled as Patsy quietly shut the door. "You sure handled it like a pro, though. Does that come from your nurse's training?"

Patsy blanched. If her fair skin could have gone any paler, Ray would have been shocked.

"What's wrong?" he asked, bewildered at how his innocent question could have upset her so, but it was obvious by her distress that he had.

"Not many people on base know about it," Patsy finally said after a silence that seemed to stretch for an eon.

Wisely, Ray didn't speak. After she sat down on the living room sofa, he sat beside her. "Go on."

"I was married about a zillion years ago. Or at least, it seems that long ago," she said softly. "We eloped in high school. I was sixteen and he was eighteen. We were so crazy in love that we didn't want to wait."

To have sex, Ray concluded, but he didn't interrupt.

"Ace worked hard and I was happy to stay at home and play at being a housewife. We had two kids right away."

That was a bombshell that Ray didn't expect. He

guessed that she and her husband had been divorced, but where were the kids?

"That's how I knew what to do with Sara. My nursing training didn't come till later." She looked off into nowhere. "I went back to school and became an R.N. just a couple of years ago," she said, her voice distant.

Ray wasn't sure he should question her, but the fact that she had kids was very important. Where the hell were they?

He waited for Patsy to go on, but for the longest time she said nothing. Just as it seemed as though she'd composed herself and was ready to continue, the glow of two headlights lit up the front window. Apparently, Rich and Jennifer were home.

She pushed herself up off the couch and headed for the door. "I'll just go and let you explain what went on to the Larsens. Come to my place when you're done."

With that, she scurried out the door and left Ray with more questions than he'd had to start with.

Chapter Seven

Patsy's heart pounded so hard as she drove herself back to her duplex a few blocks away, that if she didn't know better, she would have thought she was having a heart attack. Halfway there, she pulled over to the curb and stopped the car. She had to get herself together. She drew in several deep, cleansing breaths, then feeling a little calmer, continued the rest of the way home.

She pulled into the driveway, flung open the car door, and hurried inside as if she were being pursued by the hounds of hell.

She'd expected that she'd have to tell Ray about Ace and the children sooner or later, but she had expected it later, not sooner. Maybe if she'd had more time to think about it, she would have been better prepared.

Now, she was going to have to tell him the whole story, and she wasn't sure how Ray was going to feel about her afterward. No matter how she told him, or what she told him, there was no way to whitewash it. Her children and husband were dead. And it was her fault.

She looked around the house as if the answer to her dilemma would be there, but there was nothing different. Tripod, already settled in for the night, looked up from her bed, woofed tiredly in her direction, then settled back to sleep.

She'd have to tell Ray and hope that it wouldn't change the way he felt about her.

Patsy paced the living room, wringing her hands until she saw the lights of Ray's car through the crack between the closed drapes. Normally she would have rushed to the door, but tonight she waited. She was in no hurry to start the beginning of what would surely become the end.

He knocked lightly on the door. "Patsy, it's me. Are you all right?"

Slowly, feeling as if she were wearing magnets on her shoes and the floor were made of iron, she made her way to the door to let him in. "I guess I owe you an explanation," she said by way of greeting.

"Not if you don't want to tell me anything," Ray said, pulling her into his arms.

Patsy turned her face away from his kiss and stepped out of his arms. "No, I think I need to,"

she said. She had put it off for too long. She shut
the door, gestured toward the couch and then, tuck-
ing her feet under her bottom, seated herself in a
chair across the room. Ray adjusted his glasses,
then leaned forward expectantly.

"All right," he said carefully, his handsome face
showing his concern.

Would he demonstrate his disgust when she told
him the truth? Patsy wrung her hands together and
tried to come up with the right words. "I'm sure
you want to know where the children are," she began simply. "There's no easy way to say this.
They're dead."

Ray felt as though he'd been hit in the gut. He
gasped, but he tried to concentrate on what Patsy
said. He hadn't been prepared for this. "H-how?"
he finally managed.

"I killed them."

Again, he was not prepared for that.

"No, I didn't personally kill them," Patsy clarified, and Ray breathed a little easier. "But it was
my fault. Jesse was two years old, and Alice was
just three months. I'd had an awful day. Jesse was
going through the 'terrible two's,' and Alice had
been fussy and sick, too. So when Ace came home
from work, I told him I'd had my fill, I needed a
nap and he was in charge."

So far, it didn't sound like anything he hadn't

heard from any of the other married guys on the team, Ray thought. But, he decided, it would be better to let Patsy get the whole story out before he interrupted.

"I hadn't even fixed supper, so Ace and Jesse went off to get a hamburger from a fast-food place. Alice couldn't eat that stuff, but she always fell asleep in the car, so he took her, too. On the way back, a drunk ran a red light and plowed right into them. His SUV was no match for our small car. The kids died instantly. Ace hung on long enough for me to watch him die in the hospital."

Ray wanted to take her in his arms and hold her and tell her that it wasn't her fault, that she couldn't have helped it, but she wasn't finished.

"He asked me if I'd forgive him…" She looked off into space again, then slowly went on. "How could he ask me that when it was clearly my fault?" Her voice broke, her face crumpled, and she wept into her hands. "I told him that there was nothing to forgive. If I hadn't sent them away, they wouldn't have died."

Feeling even more helpless than he had when he'd been dealing with the fussy baby earlier in the evening, Ray did the only thing he could think to do. He went to her.

He knelt on the floor beside her chair, and pulled her up to him. She resisted him at first, but finally she turned and allowed him to take her in his arms, stroke her back and provide what meager comfort he could give.

He sat on the floor in front of the chair with Patsy—so small, so defeated—cradled in his arms and listened to her mourn her children, her husband, her family, until she finally cried herself out.

"PATSY, ARE YOU ASLEEP?"

She wasn't. She had been lying in Ray's arms, her head against his chest, listening to his strong, steady heartbeat and wondering why he hadn't pushed her away and left her alone in her misery. Yet, she was happy that he hadn't, glad that he'd stayed with her.

"No."

"Maybe it's time for you to go to bed," he said gently, and Patsy knew there was nothing sexual in his suggestion. He was such a caring man, and every additional day that she knew him, she wondered why he was interested in her.

"I don't think I could sleep," she said. "And I don't want to be alone." Patsy was testing him, she knew. If he left her now, she'd know it was over.

"I'll stay with you until you fall asleep, and then I'll go," Ray said, shifting so that he could get up. He climbed to his feet, then bent and offered her his hand. "Come. You need your rest."

Patsy took his hand and struggled to her feet. She stumbled and Ray took her in his arms and held her for a moment, then he guided her slowly to her room.

He'd never been in her room before, Patsy realized, but he knew just where to go. Not that there were that many options in her two-bedroom duplex. He led her to the bed, switched on the lamp and pulled down the coverlet. Then he sat her down on the bed and knelt to remove her shoes.

"Lie down," he said and Patsy complied, wondering at the gentleness with which he was treating her as he pulled the covers over her and tucked her in.

She didn't deserve this, but she wanted so much to have him there. She wanted him so much.

Then he lay down beside her, on top of the covers, and placed his hand, so warm, so alive, on her hip. "Now, go to sleep," he said. And surprisingly, she did.

IT WAS STILL DARK when Ray felt a slight shifting of the mattress and a movement at his side. He turned and watched as Patsy slowly lifted the sheets and crept out from beneath the covers. She stopped in front of the window and adjusted the blinds. She remained there, watching as the night slowly became day. He, in turn, watched the light slowly reveal her face. She appeared to have reached some sort of inner peace.

Ray continued to watch, in Patsy's bed, until she sighed and turned.

"Are you all right?" Ray whispered.

She started, drew a quick breath, and stopped, her hand pressed against her upper chest. "I didn't know you were awake," she said.

"I didn't want to disturb you. You seemed so lost in thought."

"Memories, you mean?"

"Yeah," Ray said huskily. "You didn't answer my question. Are you okay?"

Patsy shrugged and made a wry face. "As well as can be expected, I suppose."

Ray reached for her, and Patsy came to him, taking his hand and sitting on the edge of the bed. The mattress dipped with her scant weight, and Ray rolled slightly toward her. "It was not your fault, Patsy Pritchard," he told her firmly. "You didn't make that man drink too much. You couldn't have known that he'd be at that particular intersection at that specific moment. You didn't give him his car keys and tell him to drive."

Patsy sniffed, but she seemed to understand and accept, what he was saying.

"You are not guilty of anything except being a normal mother and wife." Ray pulled her down to the bed and drew her close to him. He pressed a kiss to her forehead and stroked her sleep-tousled hair. He wanted so much for her to know that he cared.

And that he understood.

"It was nothing but chance. Pure, awful, bad luck," Ray added to make his point. "Would you like to tell me about them?" he asked her gently.

She was quiet for a long time, then Ray heard a half sob. "I miss them so much," she whispered.

"And you should, but it would help for you to talk about them." Ray swallowed. He wasn't a psychologist, but he'd taken enough psychology courses in school to know that it wasn't good to suppress emotions. Still, it was obvious that Patsy had held her feelings inside for so long, she'd have a hard time letting them go. "I am a good listener," he offered.

When Patsy still didn't comply, Ray tried again. "Tell me about Ace."

She did.

THE SUN WAS WELL UP in the sky by the time Patsy finally finished her story. She couldn't believe that she had told Ray as much as she had, but the telling had been cathartic. For so long, she had held everything in, afraid that talking would open a Pandora's box of guilt and recriminations that she'd been unwilling to let loose. Maybe, she should have done this a long time ago, she mused.

"I have pictures," she found herself volunteering. She'd stopped looking at them long ago because every time she did all the pain and grief came rushing back. Now that Ray had helped her exorcize her demons—though she'd hardly call her darling Alice and Jesse demons—she thought she might be able to do it.

"I'd love to see them," Ray said, stretching as he rose from the floor where they'd finally wound up, sitting side by side, backs against the rumpled bed. He reached down and offered her his hand.

He'd laid his glasses on the bedside table sometime during the night, Patsy noticed. His polo shirt was untucked and rumpled from sleep, and a dark smudge of beard darkened his cheek. He radiated strength, confidence and vitality. Patsy took his hand and allowed him to help her to her feet.

Ray's hand felt warm and strong, and it sent shivers of delight running from Patsy's arm to her heart though they'd held hands many times before. How had she happened to get so lucky to get the chance to know him? How fortunate for her that Aunt Myrtle had bought him at the bachelor auction. She chuckled at the thought of it.

"That's beautiful to hear," Ray said quietly. "Almost like music."

"What?"

"Your laughter." Ray touched her cheek. "And that smile's not too shabby, either." He stroked her skin and Patsy, greedy for more of his touch, leaned in to his caress.

"Thank you," she finally murmured. What did you say to the man who had single-handedly changed your life? By doing nothing but listening.

"The pictures are in here," Patsy said, reluctantly pulling away from Ray's caress. She could stand there all day and feel him stroking her, but for some reason she wanted to—no, had to—look at her family album. It had been so long. Still holding his hand, she led the way to the hall closet, then opened the door.

"Up there?" Ray pointed to the stack of books on the top shelf.

Patsy nodded. Would she be able to do it? she wondered as Ray reached up and collected the pile of albums she'd all but thrown up there when the mere sight of them had caused her so much pain.

The stack teetered and the top album slipped. Patsy caught it. To her surprise, it just felt like an ordinary book, something she touched every day. Still, this was special: the record of her family almost to the last day.

She rubbed away the accumulated dust of years

of disuse and neglect and then pressed it to her chest. It seemed to throb with life and love.

Ray took her elbow. "We'll go into the living room and sit down." He steered her into the other room, sat on the couch and drew her down to sit on the cushions beside him.

"Are you okay?" he asked again, as Patsy savored the anticipation of seeing the dear faces she hadn't been able to look at, but hadn't been able to forget, either. "You don't have to do this."

Smiling softly, Patsy shook her head. "Yes, I do. I want to. And I thank you for bringing me to this point." She flicked a speck of dust off the dark green fabric cover, then she drew in a deep breath and slowly lifted the cover and opened the book.

On the first page was a photo of her and Ace, the two of them dressed up for the senior prom. She smiled. Lord, they looked so young.

"Wedding pictures?" Ray asked, breaking the reverent silence.

Patsy laughed, and surprisingly, it felt good. "I guess this is the closest thing to a wedding picture I've got, but that's from Ace's senior prom. He and I eloped on prom night."

"Right," Ray said. "Good-looking couple."

"Yes, we were," Patsy agreed, turning the pages, exclaiming delightedly as each picture brought back another memory. How wonderful to be able to see them all and not to hurt.

She turned to Ray. "Thank you so much for bringing me to this moment. I didn't think I would ever get here." Not that she'd tried in recent years.

She was so glad that Ray Darling had come into her life. So happy that he'd helped her finally come to the realization that there was more to living than her job.

How could life get any better?

THOUGH PATSY had seemed to weather the emotional storm of last night and this morning, she still might need him, Ray thought. So he fed Tripod, let her outside, and now he was in the kitchen frying bacon while Patsy showered herself awake.

How he wished he were in there beside her.

But, considering all that Patsy had been through in her life, not to mention, last night and this morning, there was no way he would rush her. He'd wait for her to make the first move, and if she never did, he'd just have to live with it.

He put some coffee on, and the air was soon filled with the fragrant aroma of morning. He might have slept some last night in Patsy's bed, but he hadn't slept well. Most of the night he had lain there and watched her sleep, and it had been one of the most arousing experiences he'd ever had.

This morning, his body ached as though he'd spent the night in a sleeping bag on the rocky floor of some chilly Middle Eastern desert. Not that he'd ever been to a Middle Eastern desert; he was just using his imagination.

And his imagination had been working overtime recently, thinking about what he'd been missing in his life—not the desert experience, but Patsy. He poured himself a mugful of dark, rich coffee and brought it to his mouth. He took a sip and swallowed.

"Oooh, it smells wonderful in here," Patsy exclaimed as she entered the kitchen.

Ray hadn't heard her come in, and he looked up, startled. She was wearing some sort of cotton robe, damp in places and so thin that it showed off the figure beneath as if she were wearing nothing at all. She was toweling her hair dry as though it were an everyday event to walk into a room half-naked in front of a man.

A very interested man. He'd imagined what she would look like, but his imagination had not come anywhere close to the perfection in front of him.

He put his mug down and forced his attention back to the cooking bacon. "This is about done. I'll just drain the bacon, and cook up the eggs, and then we can eat."

Patsy padded over to the coffeepot and poured

herself a mugful. Then she opened the fridge and took out some milk. She put some in her mug and brought it to her lips. As Ray had, she breathed in the aroma before drinking. He felt a stirring in his loins and he did what he could to discourage any outward demonstration of his ardor. That was proving more difficult by the minute.

Leaning against the counter, Patsy sipped her coffee and watched him as he poured off the grease and introduced the eggs to the pan. They were both rewarded by the satisfying sizzle as the eggs hit the hot grease.

"You know, a woman could get used to this," Patsy murmured, watching him over the rim of her upraised mug as he expertly scrambled the eggs.

"Used to what?"

"Having a man cook for her." She put her mug down and arched a pale eyebrow, her blue eyes wide with curiosity. "How did you get so familiar with the workings of a kitchen?"

"I'm familiar with the feeling of being hungry, therefore, I'm familiar with the experience of filling me up," Ray answered flippantly. He shrugged. "I eat, therefore, I cook."

"What's your specialty?" Patsy asked as she reached into a cabinet for plates.

"Microwave dinners, actually," Ray said. "I get home so late most days that I don't have time to get into anything too complicated. I am getting fairly proficient in the art of grilling, though.''

"You'll have to show me some time," Patsy said. "I either burn stuff or take it off too rare.''

"Well, for now, you'll just have to make do with eggs.'' Ray scraped the scrambled eggs onto the plates, added the bacon and some toast and they adjourned to the table to eat.

IT HAD BEEN SO LONG since Patsy had sat across a breakfast table from a man that it should have felt strange, but with Ray, it felt familiar, right. She loved his rumpled, unshaven look, his glasses spotted with bacon splatters. In fact, it had her thinking about things, other than what was on the plate in front of her.

He must have noticed the grease on his glasses, for he took them off, blew warm fog onto them, then rubbed at them with a paper napkin. He put them back on and watched her eat.

Patsy ate her breakfast, brunch really, and wondered what would happen next.

"You are a real lifesaver,'' she declared as she pushed her plate away. "I hate to wait for breakfast to cook, so I usually end up eating cereal.''

"Then why did you have all the proper ingredients stocked in your refrigerator?'' Ray countered.

Patsy had to laugh. "Oh, I always plan to use

the stuff. I regularly resolve to eat better, but then I usually end up going through the fridge once a month or so, tossing the old stuff out, and starting fresh. You're lucky, I just did that last week.''

Ray swallowed what he was chewing and looked at her. ''Thank goodness for small favors,'' he said dryly. ''I don't suppose you have any steaks stashed in there, do you?''

''Not hardly. There's not much of anything to cook for two.'' Patsy wondered if, by his words, she was correct in assuming that he wanted to spend the rest of the day with her, that he might want to stay long enough to grill those steaks he'd mentioned.

''Why don't you go take a shower while I clean up the kitchen?'' she asked. ''After all, you cooked. The least I can do is straighten everything up.''

''I can go home and shower, if you think you'll be all right.''

Patsy felt a twinge of disappointment. ''I was hoping that later, you would show me your grilling technique. You did ask about whether I had any steaks here.''

''I'll tell you what,'' Ray said, ''I'll go home and change, then I can come back with some steaks and I'll give you that grilling lesson you requested.''

''Works for me,'' Patsy said, smiling. For a weekend that had started out pretty awful, it seemed to be turning out pretty well.

Chapter Eight

Patsy sat in a lawn chair in the backyard, Tripod dozing comfortably at her feet, and watched as Ray prepared another meal for her. She smiled. How long had it been since she hadn't had to fix a meal for herself? She couldn't remember the last time. Well, except for that dinner at Aunt Myrtle's.

She hadn't even been certain that Ray would return after what she'd put him through last night. That he had, told her more than anything he could have put into words.

She liked that.

More than that, she liked Ray. It felt so good to have someone in her life, not someone who was linked to her by blood, but someone who chose to be there. Aunt Myrtle might have fixed them up, but Ray had been the one to keep the relationship going. He'd been the one who'd pressed and pushed and taken every opportunity to insinuate himself into her life. And she was so glad that he had.

The aroma of well-seasoned meat wafted through the air and she moistened her lips. "Are you sure I can't do something to help you?" she called.

Ray turned, grinned, and said, "No, you take care of people all the time. When was the last time anybody took care of you?"

Funny how they'd both been thinking the same thing. Patsy shrugged. "I don't know. But I love that you're doing it now."

After so many years of being afraid to remember, afraid to care, Patsy reveled in the novelty of having someone else to think about. The only regret she had was that Ray could leave her at a moment's notice.

Not by choice, but because of the very business he was in. Radar was in one of the most dangerous career fields in the air force. Not only could he be hurt or killed in a battlefield situation, but even his training exercises were riskier than those of most of the servicemen she ministered to. She had lost count of all the broken bones, lacerations and other such injuries she'd witnessed at the clinic that had happened as a result of routine training right here on base.

But, she forced herself not to dwell on that. She tried to make herself think of only the here and now. Ray was here now, and she enjoyed being with him. Wasn't that enough?

For now, maybe, it was.

Patsy leaned over to pet the dog, and thought again about how domestic the scene felt.

A woman could get used to this.

Patsy leaned back in her chair and smiled. Instead of running away from the possibility of a real relationship, as she'd done for years, she actually wanted to stay for more.

RAY SPEARED THE STEAKS and dropped them on a platter then used the spatula to remove the vegetables he'd grilled. He might not be a gourmet cook, but the couple of things that he did cook were better than average, if he said so himself.

He turned to where Patsy was relaxing in the dappled shade, the dog at her feet, and announced, "Soup's on. Come and get it."

Patsy looked up and slanted a sly smile in his direction. "Now just how did you manage to cook soup on the grill?" she asked. "Didn't the broth keep running through the grid, putting the coals out?"

Setting the plate on the picnic table in front of Patsy, Ray did not dignify the silly question with an answer. There had been a time when he wouldn't have understood that simple flirtatious remark.

There was a time when he would have tried to explain.

Thank God he'd learned more than warfare since joining the air force. "I'll let you figure that out all by yourself," he said, taking a seat.

"No, thank you," Patsy said. "I'll just eat." She picked her chair up and hurried with it to the table. "It smells delicious."

"You know, there was a time when I would have taken your statement about the broth literally," Ray said, and Patsy arched an eyebrow. How could such an intelligent man misunderstand a remark like that?

"I was a smart kid," Ray went on. "Remember when I told you'd I'd gone to the University of Washington?"

Patsy nodded. "You clammed up about it, and I tried not to pry. I was curious, though. Did you get into trouble there or something?"

"No," Ray said. "I was too young to get into trouble."

"Too young? Just how old were you when you graduated?"

"Seventeen."

Patsy almost choked on the piece of steak in her mouth. She grabbed for her glass of soda and took a big swallow. "You *were* a smart kid."

"One eighty IQ," he said simply. "I taught myself to read before I even entered kindergarten, and my parents were afraid that I'd be lost in a classroom of thirty kids, so they decided to home school me. My mom was a teacher, but I exceeded her abilities by the time I was twelve. That's when they sent me to a private high school known for academic excellence, but I tested out of there in two years and went on to college when I was fourteen.

"I knew all sorts of book stuff, but I didn't have a clue about the world. I'd never played in a ballgame, been on a date or done a lot of the things that other kids take for granted."

"You led an awfully sheltered life, then," Patsy concluded. "And you were too young to date college girls and learn about flirting and how to talk to people your own age."

Ray shrugged. "I never had the chance to spend much time around people my own age. Until I joined the air force, my life was nothing but adults and books and school."

"How sad," Patsy murmured. "But you seem pretty caught up now."

"That's why I joined the air force. I wanted to learn how to be a real guy." He sliced off a piece of steak, popped it into his mouth and chewed. "You can't learn that from books," he said, his mouth still full.

"No, I guess not." There was a lot to be said

about good, practical experience. And Ray had certainly made up for lost time, Patsy couldn't help thinking. But then, maybe his experience in school had made him a quick study. A very quick study, she amended. She glanced across the table to the strong, handsome man sitting there. And thank goodness he was.

"My parents are still not speaking to me," he said.

"For heaven's sake, why not?" Any parent should be proud of the man Ray had become.

Ray shrugged. "I was accepted to MIT for graduate studies in mathematics, but instead I enlisted in the air force. I think they had hopes of me becoming the youngest Ph.D. on record or something."

"But that obviously wasn't what you wanted for yourself," Patsy concluded. "Even if the Massachusetts Institute of Technology is a very prestigious school and difficult to get in to." She reached across the table and took his hand.

"They refused to understand that." He closed his hand over Patsy's and she felt a thrill of warmth and comfort from it. Funny, she'd offered her hand as a gesture of reassurance to Ray, but he'd made her feel good, as well.

"I think they're afraid I'll do something reckless like get myself killed and waste their investment."

"I hope you straightened them out on that," Patsy said, showing her indignance at his family's presumption.

"I tried. They wouldn't listen."

He was trying to be nonchalant about it, but Patsy could see the hurt in his eyes.

"I finally quit trying."

There wasn't much more Patsy could say, but now she certainly could understand why Ray had seemed so different from the other men who came through the clinic. And why she had liked him so quickly.

They were both outsiders. They both had emotional baggage to carry. He'd helped her with hers. Maybe some day she could return the favor.

RAY HAD FINISHED his own steak, and now he sat back and watched as Patsy polished off hers. "I do enjoy watching a woman eat," he said, hoping he wouldn't offend her.

"This woman enjoys eating," Patsy said, scraping at the skin of her baked potato. "Especially, when the food is as good as this, and she doesn't have to cook it herself. This seasoning is divine."

"That's the Secret Radar Sauce," Ray said.

Patsy arched an eyebrow and cast him a questioning look as she sliced off another morsel of meat.

"If I told you, I'd have to kill you." He slipped another scrap to the dog. "And I'd hate to have that happen."

"I'll second that," Patsy said, her mouth full. "And I don't care if you don't tell me the secret recipe as long as I can keep you around to fix it for me. The way to a woman's heart is definitely through her stomach," she declared.

Ray wondered if she actually meant it. He thought he'd be more than happy to hang around and keep her satisfied, and not just in the dining room. He loved doing things for Patsy. No, he loved Patsy. And that thought nearly knocked him out of the lawn chair.

When had love entered this equation? They hardly knew each other. Surely, it was too soon to be entertaining notions of love?

He glanced across the table to Patsy, obviously relishing every bite of the meal he'd cooked for her, and wondered what she was thinking. One thing was certain: it was far too early for broaching the topic of love with her. He would declare his feelings one day. He just wanted to be sure that those feelings were reciprocated before he did.

Patsy cut off a tiny morsel of her steak and slipped it under the table to Tripod and Ray had to smile. She tried to be tough and icy toward the guys she took care of at the clinic. If they only knew what a soft touch Prickly Patsy Pritchard really was....

RAY KISSED HER quickly on the lips, then turned to leave.

"One more, please," Patsy begged, greedy to continue experiencing the emotions she'd suppressed for so long.

He bent down to kiss her again, then stepped away. "You know, I'd love to keep kissing you," he growled huskily. "But if I do, I don't think I'll be able to force myself to leave."

"All right," Patsy complained, her tone more teasing than disappointed. "But you owe me one."

"Or two dozen," Ray added, smiling. "Don't worry. I want to keep doing this as much as you do." His smile gentled. "You know, you've had a big weekend. I don't think it would be a good idea to overdo it," he said, his voice softening. "Do you understand?"

Patsy swallowed the lump of emotion that had come to her throat at Ray's thoughtfulness. "Yes," she whispered. "I understand. But there's always next time."

"Yeah, next time," Ray echoed. "It's a date." He started to step outside, then turned back again. "I want there to be many more days for us," he said, then he stepped outside.

Patsy leaned against the doorjamb and watched as Ray climbed into the car. He switched on his headlights in the thickening twilight and Patsy stepped inside the house. She had spent almost twenty-four hours with this man and she'd enjoyed every moment, even the moments of pain because after them had come the release she had needed for such a long, long time.

Patsy parted the living room drapes and waved. She watched through the window as Ray backed his car out of her driveway, then she smiled. She stayed at the window until the twin red taillights disappeared in the distance. What a difference a day made.

Yesterday, she was still hiding her feelings about what had happened to her family. Then Ray Darling had marched into her world and had forced her to talk out the pain, the guilt she had been trying so hard to ignore. Yesterday, she had been hiding from life.

Today, she was ready to embrace it.

And all because of one man.

She smiled again, let the drapes fall back together, and turned back to the family album that she'd left untended for so long. A packet of photographs fell out, and Patsy bent to pick them up.

The glue on the envelope was sealed tight, still unopened after all this time. Patsy held the packet, turning it from front to back, side to side, trying to remember what it could contain. Finally, after several long minutes, she slid her finger under the flap and tore the packet open.

Taking a long, deep breath, for courage, Patsy supposed, she reached inside and plucked out the contents. It had been one thing to unveil the contents of the photo album with Ray there to provide support, but now she was alone. Would she be able to handle the memories? Patsy closed her eyes, and uttered a silent prayer.

Then she unfolded the protective covering from around the photos sealed within and peeked quickly inside. Patsy laughed out loud and looked again, this time longer than just a peek. Smiling, she remembered the day these photos had been taken. It had been so hard to get Jesse to sit still that she and the photographer had begun to despair of ever getting a good shot. Jesse had been suffering from such a case of the wiggles and giggles that he kept slipping off the seat. But Jesse's giggles had made Alice laugh, so they'd been able to get some great shots of the two of them.

The pictures had been taken the week before the accident, and the processed photographs had arrived in the mail the day of the funeral. No wonder she hadn't opened them.

Now, looking at them, Patsy was glad that today

she had. That had been such a happy day, and today it felt wonderful to remember the good times. She settled onto the corner of the couch, placed the album in her lap and leaned back to look through it again. There were so many good memories enclosed in that one book. Why had she deprived herself of them for so long?

Tomorrow, she was going to get a frame and she was going to put one of the pictures out so she could see it and look at it every day. She'd ignored the memory of her children for far too long. Patsy kissed her fingertip and placed it gently on the smiling faces—one then the other—of her children. "I love you," she whispered.

Then she looked up into the empty room. "Thank you, Ray Darling. Thank you for giving my children back to me."

RAY WAS STILL smiling when he loped up the stairs to his second-floor apartment. He hoped that his increasingly morose roommate would not ruin the good mood he was in.

"Well, look what the cat finally dragged in," Danny Murphey grumbled when Ray let himself in to the apartment. "You must have had one hot date."

No, Ray told himself. He would not let Danny's bad mood ruin his. "And that would be a problem, why?'' Ray said as he lowered himself to the couch where Danny had apparently been watching a baseball game.

''Depends on who it was.''

Ray chose to ignore the statement. He was pretty sure that Danny wanted to know who he'd been with, but Ray wasn't telling. His time with Patsy was too private, his feelings for her too new, to share. ''Who's winning?''

Danny ran a hand through his uncombed rusty hair, shrugged and reached for a sweating bottle of beer amid the clutter of several empties. ''Don't know. Don't care. It was on, that's all.''

''You know, man, you gotta pull yourself out of this blue funk you've been in lately. If you're not careful, you're going to screw up on the job.''

''Get off my back,'' Danny snapped. ''I'm stone-cold sober.'' He made a sweeping gesture toward the mess on the coffee table. ''This is left over from last night. You'd know that if you'd been here.''

Ray held up his hands in a gesture of surrender. ''Okay, okay. It's none of my business, anyway,''

''Got that in one.'' Danny lifted the beer to his lips and took a long swig.

''Any more where that came from?'' Ray pushed himself up and headed to the refrigerator in the cluttered kitchen. Danny really needed to pull himself together; the place was a mess. So far, Murphey had been holding his own on the squad, but he damned sure wasn't holding up his end in the apartment.

"I bought a twelve pack this morning," Danny called. "Help yourself." His tone had lightened some, and Ray took that as a good sign.

He got himself a beer, then snagged some sliced cheese, and slapped it between a couple of pieces of bread. He'd just enjoyed a wonderful meal with Patsy, but Danny's morose mood had left a sour taste in his mouth. Maybe, if he ate something, it would take the bad taste away.

And while he was chewing, he wouldn't have to talk.

PATSY HAD BEEN counting the days since her breakthrough with Ray. It had been so long since she'd actually looked forward to a Friday night that she felt almost giddy with anticipation.

Smiling, she finished her paperwork, policed the area around her desk, and switched off her computer. She'd make a quick stop to pick up her uniforms from the laundry, and then she'd be free.

She smiled again as she looked at the framed photo of the kids she'd placed on her desk.

"Cute kids," Mary Bailey, the head nurse commented from the doorway behind Patsy. "They your niece and nephew?"

"No, they're mine. They died with their father in a traffic accident a long time ago," Patsy replied simply. She'd thought that saying it would hurt, but it wasn't so bad. She felt a pang of sadness, of course, and she supposed she always would, but it was nothing compared to what she'd been carrying around, hidden inside her heart, for all these years.

"Oh," Mary said, startled. "I didn't know."

"I didn't tell," Patsy said. "It took me a long time to get over it. I'll always miss them, but I'm planning on looking ahead from now on."

Mary smiled. "I always thought you had something heavy to deal with. I'm glad you have. You seem so much happier now. It's wonderful to see the change."

"Thanks," Patsy said. She wasn't quite ready to tell Mary how she'd achieved the change. She'd walked around under a dark cloud for so long, she was afraid to let in too much light so soon.

Ray had practice with his team before their date tonight, but she wasn't going to watch this time. She'd been putting off giving Tripod a bath and the balmy afternoon temperatures made it a perfect time to get the deed done. Tripod made a mess in the bathroom, and today she'd be able to hose her off outside.

Patsy hurried through her errands, humming as she went, even picked up the gourmet dog food that

Tripod liked. She might have to give the dog a treat after subjecting her to a bath. It would be several hours before Ray was finished coaching, so she had plenty of time to anticipate their evening together.

"WHAT'S GOING ON HERE?" Ray called over the sound of frenzied barking and running water.

Patsy called from the backyard. "We're out here. Tripod is not in the mood to be bathed."

Ray opened the gate to the chain link fence and stepped into the backyard. He took one glance and had to laugh. Patsy, looking as though she'd been caught in a sudden rainstorm, was holding a rubber hose, water trickling from the nozzle. She was soaking wet, her blond hair dripping, her makeup smeared, and Tripod was doing a three-legged dance, running back and forth, seeming to taunt her mistress with playful barks. The dog was wet, muddy and far dirtier than she'd probably been to start with.

"It isn't funny, Ray Darling," Patsy declared, aiming the hose at him.

He didn't dodge it fast enough. Dripping, he dashed toward Patsy, yanking the hose from her. He got her back, the force of the water hitting her so hard that she lost her balance and sat down in a muddy puddle. "Turnabout's fair play," he declared.

Patsy shook off the water, flinging droplets everywhere. "You are not helping, Ray. Look at that dog!"

Tripod, already wet and muddy, was now rolling in a freshly turned flower bed. Her white spotted coat was now brown with dirt. She stopped, looked up, a doggy smirk on her face, then resumed her dirt bath.

"I will never get her clean," Patsy wailed.

"It doesn't look like she wants to be," Ray commented as he dashed after the muddy dog.

"Well, I want her to be, and I'm the boss," Patsy said, as Ray captured the runaway pooch. "Besides, she stinks."

"For a three-legged dog, she sure can run," Ray said, capturing Tripod and carrying the squirming animal to the wash tub. He got a good whiff. "What did she do? Run into a skunk?"

"No, that's just what she smells like if she doesn't get her weekly bath. Usually, she enjoys it." Patsy hosed down the protesting dog, washing the mud off. "Hold her while I soap her up."

"You sure you don't want to abandon this project?" Ray asked as the dog, barking at the top of her lungs, tried again to escape. "You're going to have the animal protection people coming after you."

"No, I won't," Patsy muttered determinedly. "But I *will* have a sweet-smelling dog."

FINALLY, THE DOG *WAS* clean and sweet-smelling, but Patsy couldn't say the same for Ray. She laughed at the sorry sight in front of her. "I guess we'd better cancel our dinner reservation," she said.

"Ya think?" he said dryly.

"I think," Patsy declared. "Why don't you take a quick shower, and I'll toss your clothes into the machine. I can probably scare up an old set of sweats or something for you to wear till they dry."

"It doesn't look like I have a choice," Ray said. "What about our reservation?"

"I'll cancel it. I don't think we'll make it now. You go wash." Patsy shooed him with one hand and herded Tripod into her crate with the other. "I'm not letting this clean doggie out until she's good and dry."

Ray turned to leave the kitchen, then looked back over his shoulder. His polo shirt was so wet that it clung to him and gave Patsy a perfect view of his well-defined muscles. "What are we going to do for supper?"

"Don't worry," Patsy said, an excellent, delicious, sneaky idea forming in her mind. "You just toss your wet stuff outside the bathroom door and I'll take care of everything.''

And you, she thought but didn't say out loud.

RAY STOOD IN THE SHOWER behind the feminine-looking curtain and relished the feel of the warm water sluicing over his body. Who would have thought that one little dog could get a guy so wet and muddy?

He wished he had a change of clothes here, but the sweats would do for now. He was used to making do. He'd spent many a night in the field in dirty, wet clothes. Dry sweats would be like heaven compared to wet BDUs. And using Patsy's well-appointed bathroom was not a hardship at all.

He scrubbed himself clean with soap that was definitely too womanly for his taste, then lathered his face with foam from a can of more floral-scented stuff. He sure hoped that nobody from the team would get a whiff of him while he still reeked of it.

He scraped at his five o'clock shadow as best he could, using the pink razor Patsy had left on the edge of the tub. He was shaving blind because he couldn't see what he was doing, so he ran his fingers over his face, checking for rough spots. Then satisfied, he rinsed the remaining soap off the razor.

As he reached for the taps to turn off the water,

a draft of cool air moved the curtain. Ray shivered in reaction to the chilly breeze. Had the air conditioner come on?

"Don't turn the water off," Patsy purred. "I'm muddy, too."

Ray dropped the razor and turned quickly. A very feminine hand appeared at the edge of the shower curtain. Patsy pulled the curtain aside and stepped into the tub.

Ray drew in a short, quick breath.

She was delightfully, beautifully, naked. And the few smudges of dirt still on her face just made her look even more appealing.

"I thought I'd take the opportunity to get you to help me scrub my back," Patsy murmured.

Chapter Nine

"Actually, washing was not what I had in mind," Patsy said in the sultriest voice she could muster as Ray, looking very flustered and very interested, reached for the washcloth. She slid freshly soaped-up hands over Ray's broad, hard chest, until the swirls of his chest hair were foamy with soap once again, and his skin slick. Then she pulled him to her.

"I—I guess not," Ray stammered, and it tickled Patsy to see him so thoroughly flustered.

"I thought you hard-core, commando types were always prepared for action," she whispered, pressing her breasts against him.

"Yes," he said. "I'm pretty certain I can manage to rise to the occasion," he said, his voice strong and confident now that he'd gotten over the surprise she'd sprung on him.

"Well," Patsy murmured huskily, glad that she'd

come up with a way to show Ray what she wanted and to make him an offer he was unlikely to refuse. "Kiss me and show me," she said.

Much to her delight, he did.

Soaping up the washcloth once again he gently washed the mud off her. The cloth lingered over the sensitive parts of her anatomy. He concentrated on her breasts, bringing her nipples to rock-hard attention. Then he moved lower, and soon he had her body screaming for completion.

Patsy's breath came in short, panting gasps, and she didn't think she could bear to wait a moment longer. She wrapped her wet arms around him and pulled her to him again, offering her mouth, her lips, her self to him.

He accepted her invitation and showed her just how much he wanted her. He kissed her, caressed her, and drove her nearly mad with wanting.

Then, shivering as the water from the shower ran cold, his hard desire throbbing against her, he lifted her slippery, cold body, carried her into her bedroom and showed her just how much he wanted her.

That and so much more.

DARK HAD FALLEN by the time Ray woke up in Patsy's bed. Light from the streetlamp outside the bedroom window peeked between the slats of the venetian blinds and painted an interesting pattern on the bed. This time they weren't in their clothes as they had been the week before. This time they were under the covers together. Deliciously nude.

He yawned, and Patsy did the same, stretching with slow and languid grace like a cat rising from a nap in front of a warm fire. And like a cat, Patsy was wearing an I-got-the-canary expression.

"Happy?" Ray asked, wondering if his question would break the mood.

"Ecstatic," Patsy replied, rolling toward Ray and wrapping her arms around him. There was nothing sexual in her action, but Ray was instantly aroused.

"Mmmm," Patsy murmured. "Just what I like, a man who comes to attention for me."

Ray pulled her closer so that their bodies were touching, skin to skin with no space between them. "I aim to please," he said.

Patsy laughed, and the gentle motion did nothing to quench his desire. "Please me, then."

This time, Ray meant to take it slow and easy. The first time, they'd come together in a heated explosion. It had been over far too quickly, and this time he wanted the feeling to last. He wanted everything to last.

He hadn't planned on falling in love. The realization that he had all but knocked him off his feet. Marriage and family were not in his immediate plans. Until now he'd put other things, like Officer

Training School, first. Now, he thought, he might just have to revise his plans.

That could come later, though. For now, he had a woman to please, as well as himself. He angled himself away from her delectably smooth body and bent to nuzzle Patsy's neck. He smiled contentedly as she purred with delight. He kissed her throat, the little hollow at the base of her neck, her silky, alabaster skin, and slowly explored her from the top of her head to the tips of her unpainted toes.

He savored the fragrance of Patsy's flowery, feminine soap—much better on her than him—that mingled with the musky scent of lovemaking. Her fair skin was so soft, so smooth, so delicate...

Ray kissed her, he caressed her and made her tremble in his arms. Then, just when he was certain he could hold off no longer without exploding, Patsy murmured, "If you don't make love to me right now, Ray Darling, I might burst into flames."

"Can't let that happen, now can we?" Ray whispered huskily as he positioned himself over her and gently kneed her legs apart.

"Now, Ray Darling. Now," she all but commanded. "Make us one."

Ray entered her, and then he was in no condition to think.

The rest was instinctual, natural, timeless. She accepted him, and he filled her, rocking and thrusting until he had her arching eagerly to meet him. He felt her contractions ripple through her and around him as she came bucking and moaning with satisfaction. Only then did he allow himself to tumble, out of control, head over heels, heels over head, over the edge.

PATSY LAY, DROWSY, SATED and comfortable, entwined in Ray's arms, her head pillowed on Ray's chest.

Then her stomach grumbled and spoiled the silence. Quickly, Patsy pressed her hand against her complaining belly, and hoped that Ray had not heard it.

"Suffering from borborygmus, I hear," Ray dead-panned dryly.

Patsy sat up in bed, clutching the sheets to her chest. "I am so embarrassed that you heard my stomach growl," she wailed.

"Why? It's a natural function," he said.

"Sure, so is flatulence, but I don't want to do it in public. And certainly not at a time like this." Patsy felt the heat of her embarrassment as it stained her cheeks. "I could just die."

Ray laughed. "Don't do that. Why don't I just feed you instead?" He pushed himself up and swung his legs over the side of the bed and glanced at the display on the bedside clock. "I guess it's too late to call for a pizza," he said.

"You're right about that," Patsy said, looking as well. "I don't know anybody who delivers after midnight."

"You seemed to like my cooking well enough last time," Ray said. "I could whip something up."

"I like this better," Patsy murmured, feeling decidedly annoyed at her traitorous stomach. But she was hungry. And not just for Ray. They'd tumbled out of the shower and into the bed and completely forgotten about dinner.

Ray had already wrapped a towel around his middle and strode toward the door. "I expect my pants are dry by now. I'll get dressed."

"Not unless Tripod put them in the dryer," Patsy said, glad that she wouldn't have to stop looking at him quite so soon. "I didn't get them out of the washing machine before we…" She shrugged. "You know."

"That I do," Ray said, laughing. "I'll toss them into the dryer while I toss together something to eat."

"Omigosh." Patsy tumbled out of bed, tripping over the jumble of bedclothes. "I completely forgot to feed Tripod, too." She scrambled out of the tangled bedclothes and looked for her robe.

"Take your time, Patsy. I'll feed her. You get

dressed,'' Ray said. ''Not that I don't like that outfit you're wearing right now,'' he added, eyeing her alabaster skin appreciatively.

''I rather like yours, too,'' Patsy said. ''Now, go before we get distracted again.''

THEY DID GET DISTRACTED again, but not until Ray had fed the dog and made a couple of delicious omelettes. Now, both types of hunger satisfied, he lay in Patsy's bed once again, holding her close against his heart.

A guy could definitely get used to this, he thought as he felt her body shift and heard a contented sigh.

He caressed her velvety smooth skin and wondered just how he—the guy least likely to get a date for most of his life—had managed to get so lucky. It had definitely been a red-letter day for him. He might not be a legendary ladies' man like his roommate, Danny, was reputed to be, but he was pretty sure, he'd satisfied Patsy in every way.

It was amazing what a bright man could learn from books, he thought with a smile. He'd read the *Kama Sutra* long before he'd had the opportunity to practice what he'd learned. Between that and several other sex manuals he'd managed to get his hands on, he'd learned plenty. He was pretty sure that no woman he'd ever slept with had gone away unsatisfied. Even if he could count his encounters on one hand.

He raked his fingers through Patsy's silky, blond tresses and smiled with satisfaction. If he had his druthers, he would never sleep with anyone else.

He bent to kiss the top of Patsy's head. Then, satisfied that all was well, he joined her in deep, contented sleep.

THE SUN WAS HIGH in the sky when Patsy woke, lying spoonlike in Ray's arms. This morning, she felt delightfully satisfied and just a little sore. It had been a very long time since she'd spent a night making love, and though she'd enjoyed every moment of it, she suspected she was going to need a long soak in the tub tonight. Still, that was worth the feeling of well-being she basked in this morning.

"Ah, I see you're awake."

"Um-hmm," Patsy murmured, loathe to rouse from her delicious state of contentment. "How long have you been up?"

"Not too long," Ray said, his voice husky. "I've been watching you sleep."

"Oh, that must have been exciting," Patsy said, twisting around to face him. His face was rough with morning stubble, and there was definitely an interested gleam in his eyes. She kissed him quickly and rolled out of his arms.

"How soon they forget," Ray protested.

"Nothing personal," Patsy said, gathering the sheet around her. "But, I'm a little out of practice at this," she said, hoping she wouldn't have to go into detail.

"Oh, the equipment is a little sore, then?"

Patsy felt herself blushing. "Yes, you could put it that way." She glanced at him over her shoulder. "It was wonderful, though. Really."

"I'll second that," Ray said, pushing himself up. He reached for the clothing that they'd taken out of the dryer, folded and laid carefully on a chair before they'd gone back for seconds. No, thirds.

Patsy wondered if this was going to be the end of it. They still had the whole day to spend together, if Ray wanted to. Of course, there was a ball game later. He'd have to go by then.

"I did promise to give you another grilling lesson," Ray said, breaking into Patsy's thoughts. "Come on. Get dressed. We'll go by my apartment so I can change clothes, and then we'll go out for breakfast, and then we'll shop for lunch." Ray already had his pants on and was on his feet, buttoning his trousers.

Patsy padded to her dresser and pulled out a fresh pair of shorts and a halter top. Smiling, she murmured, "Food, food, food. I guess you need fuel to keep your strength up."

Ray just laughed again as he bent to pull on his socks. "Wouldn't want you to tire out, either," he said, slipping into his shoes. "After all, you're the one who's feeling the effects."

"Don't remind me," Patsy grumbled as she slipped her bare feet into sandals. Hopping on her right foot to pull the left shoe on more snugly, she said, "I'm hungry. Let's go."

"Don't you think you should comb your hair?"

Patsy glanced at her reflection in the mirror. The woman who looked back at her wore a pleased and rosy expression in spite of her irritation at having to get up and go. But her flushed face in combination with her sleep-tousled hair would make it plain to anyone who looked that she had been loved and loved well.

She yanked a brush off the dresser and began to pull it through her hair.

RAY LOPED UP THE STAIRS to his second-floor apartment, Patsy following close behind. He hadn't seen Danny's car in the parking lot, so he assumed that it was safe to bring Patsy up.

"Why is it that you didn't want your roommate to be here?"

Ray shrugged as he inserted his key in the lock,

and he hoped the place didn't look as bad as it usually did. "He's just been out of sorts since the bachelor auction, and I don't think it would be a good idea to flaunt us in front of him."

"Wasn't he auctioned the same night?"

"Yep, and he has refused to discuss what went on with his date," Ray said as he pushed the door open. "All I know is that it didn't go well."

The living room was okay. Danny had left the stereo on, but whatever he'd been playing had ended. Only the power light still burning showed that he'd been there. Ray crossed the room and switched it off. "Make yourself at home. I'll just be a minute."

He changed quickly, and when he returned to the living room, Patsy was looking at Danny's collection of Star Wars action figures, displayed on the far side of the room.

"So sad," she murmured.

"What's sad?"

"These things are still in their original packaging," she said, turning. "Toys are supposed to be played with, not put on shelves for display."

Ray hadn't really thought about it. He hadn't had that many toys as a child and the ones he'd had were of the educational variety. Now that Patsy had planted the idea into his mind, he agreed with her sentiment. "I'm sure there are children in Afghanistan or some other third world country who would love to be able to play with just one of them.''

One side of Patsy's perfect mouth quirked into a wry smile. ''Something like that,'' she said.

''Of course, they wouldn't have a clue about the story.''

''No, but they wouldn't have to make their own toys out of sticks and shell casings.'' She shook her head, an expression of infinite sadness in her eyes. ''Can you imagine being so deprived that you have to fashion a doll out of knotted rags?''

No, he couldn't. And Ray began to think that maybe his childhood might not have been quite as bad as he'd thought it had been. He had, after all, had warm clothes and real toys—even if they had been educational ones—to play with.

Ray took Patsy's elbow and led her toward the door. She turned and looked into Ray's eyes. ''Do you suppose he could be convinced to donate them to kids who really need them?''

Ray shrugged. Considering the surly mood Danny had been in recently, he didn't dare ask.

PATSY AND TRIPOD took their usual spots on the bleachers and watched while Ray gave the boys some last-minute coaching before the game began. She smiled as she watched him. He was a man who was meant to have kids, and she wondered what that would mean for the two of them.

She'd never really considered the possibility that she might have other children. Now that notion had begun to sneak into the corners of her mind.

She and Ray hadn't thought to use contraception, she realized. Though the timing wasn't quite right for anything to happen this time, it might be a possibility if they weren't careful from now on.

Brian's mom, in civilian clothes this week, sat next to her, a bag of popcorn in her hand. "Want some?" she offered.

Patsy smiled and shook her head. "Thanks, I ate earlier and I'm stuffed."

They'd grilled hamburgers, and though the meal hadn't been as elaborate as the steak they'd eaten the week before, it had been fun just preparing food together, eating together, being together.

It had been so long since Patsy had been part of a twosome that the experience was as new and fresh as it might have been if it had been a first. They'd cleaned up and hurried out to the ball park, Ray to coach, and Patsy and Tripod to cheer on the team.

"Play ball," the umpire called, and Patsy and Mrs. Williams turned their attention to the game.

RAY HAD BEEN looking forward to another evening with Patsy, but his cell phone rang in the middle of the after-game pizza, which didn't bode well. He excused himself from the hungry crowd and found a quiet corner of the patio.

His cell phone seldom rang, and that it had now worried him. The only reason he kept it at all was because his squad leader had to be able to reach him. He hoped that this was not one of those times.

He flipped the phone open and listened.

"Damn," he muttered as he switched off the phone.

"A problem?" Patsy asked when he returned to the table.

"Yeah, I gotta go. Duty calls."

Sergeant Williams had apparently also gotten a call. She had a worried look on her face, and that didn't make Ray feel any easier.

Patsy seemed to understand what was going on. "I can take Brian home, if you have to go. I don't mind."

If Ray hadn't already been half in love with Patsy before, he would have fallen in love with her then. She'd known exactly what was needed and she was prepared to step in. Of course, working in the Flight Surgeon's Clinic, she knew all about these kinds of calls.

He just hoped it was a test and not the real thing this time.

Ray pecked Patsy quickly on the lips and said

his goodbyes to the boys. He would have liked to have gotten a proper goodbye from Patsy, but there were fifteen sets of young eyes watching, not to mention assorted parents.

"See ya," was all he could say out loud.

I love you, Patsy, he said to himself.

PATSY COULDN'T HELP being in a wonderful mood a couple of days later as she entered the clinic. In fact, the song she'd heard on the clock radio when she woke up this morning played over and over again in her mind. And, in spite of not usually being musical, she found herself humming the melody to herself. The song, "The Happiest Girl in the Whole USA," just seemed appropriate.

One of the other nurses stopped her as she dropped her purse into the bottom drawer of her desk. "What has you in such a good mood this morning?"

"If I told you, Mary, I'd have to kill you," she said, repeating the mantra she'd heard so many times from the military men on base.

Mary held up her hands. "Okay," she said. "I won't pry. But it's about time."

"What's about time?"

"If I told you, you'd have to kill me," Mary quipped, then turned and hurried to her own office.

Was she that transparent? Patsy wondered, still

humming. She stopped herself, only to find the song on her lips again a few minutes later. Patsy shrugged and smiled to herself.

People might figure out why she was so happy, she told herself, but for now, the *who* was her secret. Her relationship with Ray was too wonderful, too new, to share with anyone. Not even Nancy, who was now out on maternity leave and not likely to divulge anything to anyone for the time being.

Patsy continued to hum and looked through the pile of medical records on the receptionist's desk. No one she knew.

She picked up the top file from the stack and headed out to the waiting room to call the first patient back to the intake area. As she scanned the room for the female airman whose name was listed on the folder, she happened to overhear a snatch of conversation.

"That Pritchard sure is a hot piece of property," one battle-dress uniform clad man said to the one next to him. He nudged the guy in the ribs and winked.

The man's leering attitude annoyed Patsy, but it wasn't anything she hadn't heard before. She turned away in her search for Airman Meredith Palmore.

But before she could call for the woman, another snippet of conversation reached her ears.

"Yeah," the same man said. Patsy glanced toward him and studied the name on the tape stitched above the left front pocket of his BDU. Hagarty. Didn't ring a bell.

''She's going out with Radar, you know, the guy with the B.C. glasses?''

Now Patsy had to listen. She was more interested in what they had to say about Ray than herself. She was really interested in what his squadmates thought of the man she was beginning to care so much about.

The other man nodded.

Patsy all but held her breath as she waited to hear the rest of Hagarty's statement. She leaned closer as the man lowered his voice.

Hagarty nudged the other man and went on. ''You know, in the squadron we got us a pool going on how long it's gonna take for him to get her in the sack. Want in on it? I reckon as Prickly as Pritchard is, it's gonna take him a right long time.''

Patsy's heart stopped beating. She couldn't believe what she'd just heard.

She'd believed that her growing relationship was private, just between her and Ray. And to hear strangers talking about her—no, taking bets about them—was chilling.

Her blood turned cold and her fingers went numb and she dropped the file. She turned as a possibility occurred to her. Had Radar been talking about her to his teammates in the locker room?

She glanced back over her shoulder to the two men still sitting in the waiting room.

How else could Hagarty know they were seeing each other? Surely not from her chaste outing with the baseball team. She and Ray barely went anywhere else....

Patsy had believed that what she and Ray Darling had shared was something special. Apparently, he'd just been interested in bragging rights.

How could he?

Chapter Ten

Ray and the rest of his team were on standby. The fighting in the Middle East had accelerated, and Special Operations Combat Control was being called in to secure a town that had been identified as a stronghold for the resistance to the United Nations peacekeepers, of which American forces were a part. Now, Ray was finally going to get a chance to use the skills he'd trained so hard to get. They were making ready to go at a moment's notice, and in spite of his eagerness to get into the action, Ray couldn't help but think this was not the right time to be leaving Patsy.

After taking inventory of his gear and making certain that all was in perfect order, Ray slammed his locker shut and tried to rehearse in his head what he would say to her. He'd have to go by the clinic to pick up a refill on a prescription, and he'd be sure to see her there.

He knew she would have already figured out that something was up and would not ask questions, but he wondered just how much of his feelings for her he should divulge. He let out a short, quick breath. What if it really was goodbye? Forever. Should he tell her his feelings, or would it be kinder for her never to know?

"Worried about the mission, Darling?"

Ray jerked around to see who had asked the question. Damn, he hated it when they used his name like that. But it was just Rico Scanlon. The sergeant's face showed no malice, so Ray figured he hadn't meant anything by it. He let it pass.

This time.

"No, just wondering what to tell my girl," he answered simply.

"Nothing about the mission," Scanlon warned. "Anything else is up to you."

Anything else was exactly what Ray was wondering about. He guessed he'd have to wing it.

MARY BAILEY stuck her head into the examination room where Patsy was adding notes to a file. "The next one's yours," she said. "Exam room three."

"Sure," Patsy said absently, still thinking about what she'd heard Hagarty say in the waiting room. She still hadn't talked to Ray. She was too afraid of what she might do or say. "I'll be done in a minute."

Instead of going on, Mary lingered at the door of the exam room.

"Is there something else, Mary?" Patsy asked.

The woman shook her head, hesitated, then shook it again. "Well, I wasn't going to say anything, but I guess I'm going to butt in. Something's bothering you. Do you need to talk about it?"

Patsy shook her head. "No," she said, but her tone of voice all but shouted that it was a lie. Yes, she did. She just wasn't used to confiding in others about her feelings. As betrayed as she felt, she didn't want to think that her brief interlude with Ray was over. Maybe, Mary could tell her what to do.

"I heard a couple of the men in the waiting room talking about me and my boyfriend." She drew in a deep breath. "They were speculating on how long it would take him to get me into bed," she said all in a rush to get it over with. "I feel so betrayed."

"By those men?"

"No, by R— I mean, by my boyfriend. How could he have been talking about us to them?" Patsy bit her lip to keep it from trembling.

"From what you said, the men were just speculating. If your boyfriend had talked, they wouldn't be wondering now, would they? I wouldn't jump to any conclusions.''

''But we agreed to keep our relationship private,'' Patsy said. ''If Hagarty knows, then somebody must have told him. I didn't.''

''Could he have seen you somewhere?''

''Not that I can think of. We haven't been dating that long. Mostly, I've been watching him coach his baseball team.''

''Well, there you have it, then. Obviously, somebody saw you there.'' Mary started to say something else, but another nurse called to remind them that patients were piling up in the waiting room. ''Oops, we'd best get to work.''

''Yeah, I guess you're right. I'll think about what you've said.'' Patsy closed the file she was working on and hurried to take care of the patient in examination room three. As much as she wanted to accept Mary's explanation, it still made her angry. She felt almost...violated.

''We've got to stop meeting like this,'' a familiar voice said as she stepped into the room.

''Sergeant Darling,'' Patsy said, struggling to keep her voice even, businesslike and calm. It was one thing to calmly discuss Ray with Mary, but Patsy wasn't quite ready to talk to him face-to-face. As much as what Mary had said seemed to make sense, she needed time to think about it before seeing him.

"I assume you've got a mission pending," she said coolly, though she knew full well that he did. She focused her attention on his file and did what she could not to look at Ray's handsome, darling, traitorous face. If she did, she didn't know what she'd do.

She wanted to talk to him. She wanted to slap him silly, but on the other hand she wanted to fling herself into his arms. What kind of fool was she?

She was so confused!

"Are you going to be okay about it?" Ray said, his voice laced with concern.

Patsy bit down on her lip. How could he act as though nothing was wrong? How could he continue to pretend nothing had happened, and that he actually cared?

Then again, he still didn't know she'd found out about the pool. Patsy shrugged, but the tension was beginning to give her a headache. "I have no say in the matter," she replied. "That's up to your commander," she said frostily.

Were all men such jerks? Or was it just air force types? How could he act so innocent and blameless?

"Patsy, honey. Is something wrong?" Ray reached for her, but Patsy stepped away.

She turned and tried to study his open folder, but she wasn't able to see a word on the page.

If only she'd had a little time to process what she heard, her emotions wouldn't be so raw right now. On top of her worry about his part in the upcoming campaign, it was just too much to handle....

Ray's fingers closed over her arm, but Patsy shook him off.

"How dare you?" she demanded.

"Dare what? Touch you where somebody might see us?" He held his hands up. "Okay, if you're still worried about other people finding out about us, I'll keep my hands off," he said with a slight hint of irritation.

What did *he* have to be so irritated about? *She* was the wounded party. "Fat lot of good that would do now. You know full well what I'm upset about," Patsy insisted. "Apparently, you've told everybody you know."

"About the deployment? You know darn well we're not supposed to talk about that." Ray looked at her, his expression innocent.

How could the man be so dense? Or did he really think she wouldn't give being the object of a betting pool a second thought?

"Sergeant Raymond Darling, I am so angry with you right now that I can hardly speak," Patsy finally managed through clenched teeth.

"Angry at me? Why?"

Could Ray really not know?

"We've got guys piling up in here," Dr. Brantley called from outside. "Let's keep 'em moving."

"I don't have time to discuss our personal business right now," Patsy said, struggling to keep her tone even. "I have to look over your file and then take care of the next guy."

"Fine," Ray said. "But this isn't the end of it. I need to know what has got you so fired up."

"Oh, you don't know?" Patsy said archly. "Figure it out. What could possibly have Prickly Pritchard 'so fired up?' as you so eloquently put it." Patsy quickly scanned his file.

"I have no idea. Enlighten me."

Patsy ignored him and slapped his file shut. "Your file is completely up-to-date. You can go."

Ray reached to pull his red beret out of the right thigh pocket of his BDU. "I'll leave, but you owe me an explanation for your behavior. Meet me in the snack bar at..." He glanced at his watch. "Thirteen hundred hours."

"Humph," Patsy managed, at the same time trying to squeeze back her tears.

As if.

RAY SAT IN THE BACK CORNER of the snack bar and glanced at his watch once again. It was already one-fifteen. If Patsy was coming, surely she'd be here by now.

He glanced at the clock on the wall above the cashier's station just in case his watch was wrong. Not that it was synchronized with his watch, which was set at ZULU time so that all of the parties involved in the mission, no matter where they were posted, could coordinate their efforts. Still, it was clear to him that Patsy was late. Or giving him the cold shoulder.

He looked down into his half-empty glass of soda. He'd waited this long, he might as well give her another few minutes. He still had another thirty minutes left for lunch.

The hand on the wall clock moved with maddening slowness, and still Patsy didn't come. Maybe she was busy with patients, he rationalized. After all, this was to be a major deployment. She might be working through a waiting room full of men. He'd give her a few more minutes. If she didn't make it by one-thirty, he was outta here.

Danny Murphey came in and, without an invitation, set his tray down on the table, turned a chair around and straddled it beside Ray. He glanced at the half-full glass of soda and the half-eaten burger. "Waiting for somebody?"

Ray shrugged and glanced at the clock. "Nope. Just taking every last minute of my free time," he lied, standing and picking up his tray. He didn't feel like dealing with Danny, and clearly, Patsy wasn't coming. "Don't know when I might get any more. Gotta go."

"Whatever," Danny said. "I envy you, man."

"For what?" A girlfriend—if that's what Patsy was—who couldn't bother to see him when she knew he was about to be deployed into a dangerous situation on the other side of the world?

"Getting to go on this mission. I got a training slot at Scott, or I'd be going with you," he said, his mouth full.

Ray shrugged. "Your loss is my gain," he said. It really was too bad Danny couldn't go, he thought. A mission was probably just the thing to knock him out of his self-pitying mood. In the meantime, he still didn't know what was eating Patsy Pritchard, but he was damned sure going to find out.

PATSY SAT IN HER DARKENED living room, feeling more miserable than she could ever have imagined. If she'd thought she could get away with it, she would have stayed at home until Ray's squadron finally got its marching orders, but they were already understaffed at the clinic, and a broken heart wasn't exactly a reason to call in sick. She vowed not to meet Ray, or talk to him, or listen to his flimsy excuses.

She wrapped her arms around Tripod and squeezed, hoping that feeling the warm-blooded dog's heart beating against her breast would help to fill the aching hole in her chest that was growing larger by the minute.

The doorbell rang, and Tripod wriggled out of her arms and bounced, barking at the top of her lungs, toward the door.

"No, Tripod, no," Patsy shouted firmly. She grabbed the dog, ready to put her in her crate to keep her from worrying her visitor—whoever it was—to death.

"You can open the door, Patsy. I heard you talking to Tripod. I know you're there," a familiar voice said in a tone that brooked no argument.

Ray.

Why hadn't she anticipated him showing up on her doorstep?

She let go of the dog and slowly opened the door. Had she really not expected him to come here? Had she subconsciously wanted him to come?

Tripod greeted Ray joyfully. Patsy's greeting was significantly more restrained.

Ray sank to his knees to pet the excited dog. "Oh, Tripod, I'm going to miss you when I'm away," he said. Finally, the dog settled down, and Ray looked up at Patsy.

"I don't want to talk to you," Patsy said coldly

as she closed the door. She didn't want to let Ray in, but she didn't want to air their differences in front of the neighbors, either.

"Well, I want to talk to you." He straightened so that the dog leaped on her hind legs to try to get his attention.

"What do you want?" she demanded, her tone as hard as she could make it. If she didn't harden her heart, she just might break down and cry.

"You," he answered simply.

It was the wrong thing to say. Patsy turned quickly away, blinking furiously to stem the threatening flood of tears. Her eyes burned, her lids feeling scalded, but she managed not to cry.

"The money from the bet wasn't enough? Surely you made certain you collected before you took off for parts unknown." She kept her tone icy, neutral, but she knew the hurt shone through. She kept her back to him. It was the only way she could keep the tears from falling.

"Money? What the hell are you talking about?" He grabbed Patsy's arm and jerked her around, forcing her to look at him.

Patsy shrugged him off and backed away. "You know darn well what I'm talking about. The bet about when you and I 'made' it. The pool, I guess is a better term?"

"Pool?"

"For a smart man, you sure are acting dense," Patsy said darkly.

"Well, perhaps now would be the appropriate moment for you to provide me with the details, then," Ray said, the expression on his face thunderous.

"The pool Hagarty had going to see how soon you got me into bed."

Ray looked shocked, then, after looking as if he was remembering something, nail-spitting mad.

"Who told you that?" Ray demanded, turning for the door. "I'm going to beat that Runt to within an inch of his life."

Patsy had never seen Ray so angry, and the vehemence of his wrath frightened her. She wasn't even sure *why* Ray was so mad. Was it because Hagarty had spilled the beans? Or because he'd done it in front of her?

Ray was jerking the door open.

"No! Wait!" Patsy grabbed his arm, holding him back. "What are you going to do?"

"I'm going to hurt that guy. I already decked him once, when he said something about a pool after he saw us together."

Just then Patsy remembered hearing the name Runt Hagerty and she increased the pressure on his arm. "That's right. He saw us together at the movie theater."

Ray looked away and muttered a curse. "Like I said, he said something to me about a pool shortly after that. But I thought I'd convinced him not to say anything about it. I hit him pretty hard."

Ray turned back and captured Patsy's hands in his. She didn't pull them away and that was the best thing that had happened all day. "You believe that I had nothing to do with this, don't you?" He did everything he could to telegraph the extent of his sincerity to her.

Patsy nodded and wiped her eyes. "I'm sorry. I shouldn't have jumped to conclusions. I should have asked you about it first."

"You have nothing to be sorry about, Patsy. I shouldn't have assumed I'd headed Hagarty off." Just thinking about the guys on the team discussing his ability to get Prickly Pritchard into bed made his blood boil. "How did you find out about it, anyway?"

Patsy sniffed. "I overheard him inviting some guy in the clinic waiting room in on the pool."

"Are you sure they were talking about you?" It didn't exactly help his ego that they were still taking action on the pool this very morning. Apparently, the gang had little faith in his romantic abilities....

"Prickly Pritchard and Radar," she said simply, linking her fingers with his. "There can't be two

other people on Hurlburt with those particular nicknames.''

''Damn,'' Ray muttered and then added an even
more pungent comment.

''Forget it, Ray. It's over.''

''I'm not sure I can.''

''You have to. You have to take the high road,''
Patsy insisted. ''You have to show that you're the
better man than he is.''

Patsy was right of course. He was the better man.
And he wasn't about to let Runt Hagarty make him
do anything that might keep him from achieving
everything that he'd worked so long and so hard
for. Not when he was so close. And, he had Patsy.

Patsy touched his face. ''Are you going to let it
go?''

Ray smiled. ''As long as I have you to think
about, I can forget just about anything.'' He bent
to kiss her.

''Thank you,'' she whispered just as his lips
closed over hers.

OF COURSE, they ended up in bed. Patsy wondered
why she couldn't say no to Ray. She ought to be
able to resist him. Just knowing that she'd so
greatly misjudged him meant that they weren't
there yet. That they hadn't completely given themselves to each other. Or maybe it was just her. She

was the one who couldn't truly trust him. Would she ever be able to give her heart to another man without reservation?

She sat up and tried to make out the form of the handsome man lying beside her. The room was dark save for the illuminated dial of her bedside clock radio.

A storm was coming and the air outside was still and thick and dense. Not even a flicker of light was visible through the blinds. As if to portend disaster, even the streetlamp was dark. Was that an ominous sign or a mere coincidence?

Until Ray had come storming in, Patsy had almost been relieved that their affair had ended. That way she wouldn't have to worry about him and wonder if he was safe while his unit was deployed. She wouldn't have to care.

"Patsy? Is something wrong?"

"I thought you were asleep." She drew her legs up and hugged her knees. "No, I don't think so," she answered vaguely. What could she tell him? That it would have been better if they *had* broken up? "I was just thinking."

"Yeah? Anything deep?" He touched her shoulder, and Patsy leaned toward him as he lightly caressed her.

Patsy smiled, though she knew he couldn't see it. She shook her head. "No, not so much," she lied. No sense in ruining the moment now. There would be plenty of time for that in the morning.

The mattress shifted and Patsy felt, more than saw, Ray push himself up on his elbows. He reached for her, and she leaned in to him again, ready for his caress. She was drawn to him as if to a magnet. As if their attraction were beyond her control.

"What say we just hold each other close and see what happens?" he suggested.

A shiver of delight—or was it dread?—shuddered through her. "Why not?" she said. After all, they had all night. And she wasn't sure how many more nights they'd get.

RAY HELD PATSY against him as the storm came closer. Lightning ripped through the sky and thunder rolled over and through them. It was as if nature were upset and angry about what was happening in the world.

Ray felt his need for Patsy grow as the storm's power increased. He didn't know why he was feeling this storm so intensely. All he knew was that he wanted Patsy. Not just now, but forever.

He pushed into her and she accepted him, opening her body to him, though still not her feelings. But Ray's need was all-consuming. There would be time later to discuss feelings. For now, he had to satisfy his desire.

Patsy clung to him. She arched against him, pressing her body to his almost as if she were trying to meld them together. As Ray's need became more urgent, the pressure of Patsy's fingers on his arms increased in kind. He felt her shudder as her muscles contracted and released around him, heard her mewling sound of satisfaction, and then he emptied himself into her, groaning with triumph of his own.

They lay together, warm and damp and sated, and Ray listened to the soft sound of Patsy's breathing, and their hearts beating in synchopation. He couldn't help thinking that this was the sound, the rhythm of life, of living, of love.

"Patsy?" If he didn't tell her now, Ray wasn't sure he'd ever have the nerve. "Are you awake?"

She didn't answer, and her breathing was even, rhythmic.

Ray sighed, long and low. Had he lost his chance?

A rogue flash of lightning illuminated the room and Ray caught a glimpse of her face. Her eyes were closed, and her cheeks were damp with tears.

Why would she have been weeping before falling asleep?

He'd read, once, that sometimes women felt the lovemaking experience so deeply, they were moved to tears. Had their lovemaking made her cry? Did the tears reflect her sexual satisfaction? Or were they tears of sadness because he was leaving soon?

Six weeks ago, life had been so much more simple. He'd been Radar, the guy least likely to. Now, he was a man in love with this complicated woman, and he was no closer to understanding how she felt than the day he'd had dinner with her and her Aunt Myrtle.

Six weeks ago, he'd been eager to get a chance to go on a real mission. Now he had that chance. And he did not want to go.

No, he did want to go. But, he didn't want to leave this beautiful, enigmatic woman, who provided him with more questions about her, the longer he knew her. Ray sighed again, linked his fingers together behind his head and stared into the dark night. Once, he thought he had all the answers. Now he wasn't sure he knew much about anything at all. He sure wished he did. He didn't want to think about it too much, but he knew this could be their last night together—ever.

With that heavy thought on his mind, Ray finally drifted into deep and restless sleep.

PATSY SQUEEZED her eyes together, holding back the scalding tears, and tried not to cry. She knew that Ray didn't know when to say "I love you" due to his inexperience with women. She knew he was probably waiting for her to say it first, and that he was probably desperate to hear her own declaration of love for him before he left for his mission in Taloom Kapoor.

But she couldn't do it. She couldn't bear it if another person she loved did not return. And telling Ray would make her love real.

Patsy lay awake wondering what to do. And when the first hint of daylight finally brightened the dark of night, Ray's cell phone rang.

He was up in an instant, and flipped open the cover. He listened for a moment, then switched off the phone. "I gotta go," he muttered tersely, then quickly pulled on his clothes.

Patsy rolled over and pulled the sheets up around her, more as a protective shield than for modesty's sake. She hugged her knees to her chest as she watched him dress.

She wanted so much to throw herself into his arms and cling to him, to beg him to stay, to tell him she loved him more than life itself, but she couldn't.

If they parted like friends, maybe he wouldn't be burdened with thoughts of the woman he'd left behind. Maybe he'd be better able to concentrate on the important task in front of him. Maybe that would keep him safe.

Ray tied his shoes and turned to her. He reached for her, and Patsy, trembling with emotion, tears burning behind lids already red and raw, drew in a deep, shuddering breath. "Take care of yourself," she said carefully, forcing her tone to be steady, hard.

Ray stood there for a moment, looking as though he expected her to say something else, as if he wanted to hear something more. He stood there for what seemed like an eternity, waiting for her to say the words she wanted so much to tell him.

When it became obvious that Patsy wasn't going to say anything more, Ray turned away. He looked over his shoulder. "Goodbye, Patsy," he said as he reached for the door handle. "It's been…real." Then he strode down the hall, and a moment later, Patsy heard the slamming of the door.

"I love you," she whispered, then she crumpled into a heap among the sheets and wept.

If she'd done it to protect him, to protect herself, why then did she feel so bad?

Chapter Eleven

Only the urgency of his final preparations for the pending mission kept Ray from going out of his mind. How could Patsy have done that to him?

He'd thought they had started something good. Had it just been him? Why couldn't Patsy have left him with words he could clutch to his heart during the dark and uncertain days to come? Why couldn't she have let him know, in no uncertain terms, that he had someone to come home to?

There had to be a reason for what she had done. Or not done. But, what was it?

It had to be more than the misunderstanding about the bet.

But what?

Ray slammed the door to his locker shut and hoisted his rucksack, laden with gear, onto his shoulder.

"Something wrong, Darling?"

It was Scanlon again. And this time, Ray didn't let it pass. "It's Sergeant Darling, even to you, Master Sergeant Scanlon," he replied sharply.

Fortunately, the older sergeant didn't take exception to his tone of voice. Scanlon held his hands in front of him, palms out, in a pacifying gesture. "Got that in one," he said. "I can see where being called that might get to you."

"Nice of you to figure it out," Ray muttered. "It does." Then he stalked out of the locker room.

Maybe Patsy really did care about him, but she thought it would be easier for him to go away thinking he hadn't left anything of real value behind.

Hell, maybe she'd done him a favor.

Ray laughed bitterly. Yeah, right.

Considering the excruciating ache in the middle of his chest, Ray figured Patsy hadn't done a particularly good job of it.

THEY HADN'T EXACTLY broadcast a timetable, but it didn't take much detective work for Patsy to figure out just exactly when the troops were going to leave. C-130 transport planes were massing on the ramps, and the atmosphere on the base was tense.

They were leaving soon.

Maybe it was foolish of her, but she had to see Ray one last time, even if he didn't know she was there. So, she stood in the shadows of the Base

Operations Building and watched as several groups of men assembled on the ramp.

Of course, the only men that interested Patsy were the ones wearing the distinctive scarlet berets. It was one of those men who had stolen her heart.

Patsy pressed her hand against her breast to still her rapidly beating heart. Would she be in trouble if she got caught lurking around in the shadows? Or would nobody care?

She searched the forest of men for one man, and one man alone. Ray Darling. Her darling sergeant.

Then she saw him. And she did everything she could to memorize the sight of him.

Maybe he didn't know that she was there. Maybe he would never know, but she would. She would know that she'd been there to telegraph her love.

And she hoped that he'd feel it.

Ray didn't know why he suddenly felt the urge to look back at the Base Ops building, but something drew his eyes to the shadow on the far side of the building. Something, someone, moved there. Maybe it had just been his imagination, but he had felt her there.

Patsy.

Patsy had come to see him off.

She did care.

She had just been afraid to show it.

He gazed into the shadows as long as he could,

certain he could just see the outline of her slim figure. He couldn't bring himself to believe that the feeling, the glimpse, had been his imagination.

Patsy was there. Ray focused his gaze toward the figure in the shadows and concentrated on visualizing her perfect, dear face. He pictured her cool blue eyes, the soft pink lips, the wisps of flaxen hair he loved to play with when they were alone.

He imagined that she was doing the same.

Then he mouthed the words neither of them had said. "I love you, Patsy. I love you." He didn't know if she saw, but he suddenly knew it was desperately important for him to make the effort.

"HAVE YOU HEARD from your young man?" Aunt Myrtle asked out of the clear blue sky one Saturday afternoon when she appeared on Patsy's doorstep, doing what Patsy referred to as one of her "surprise inspections."

Patsy was in shorts and a T-shirt, wearing no makeup and her hair was pulled back in a careless ponytail. Aunt Myrtle was dressed to the nines like a large bird of paradise. Patsy was certain that Aunt Myrtle would give her demerit points for her lack of effort, but she didn't really care. Myrtle's demerits meant nothing to her.

Ray did.

Myrtle shook her head and tut-tutted as she stepped inside.

Patsy averted her eyes and looked down at her bare feet, another no-no in Aunt Myrtle's etiquette book, and tried to prevent her feelings from showing on her face. "No. Why should I?"

"Why, indeed?" Myrtle answered, making Patsy feel worse than she already did. "I thought he was quite smitten with you and you with him. Was I mistaken?" Patsy followed as her aunt bustled into the living room, her suitcase-sized pocket book tucked under her arm. "You were so reticent about talking about your date, that I concluded that it went just fine. After all, you have always been quite vocal about how unpleasant the dates I've arranged for you have been." She tut-tutted as she looked around the room, cluttered with newspapers and Tripod's toys.

At least, the dog was outside at the moment, Patsy thought irrelevantly as Myrtle gingerly lifted up a pile of newspapers and settled down carefully on the couch, frowning at the television blaring war coverage from the all-news channel.

Patsy hadn't felt like doing much of anything since Ray had left for Taloom Kapoor except dress and go to work. To tell the truth, she hadn't really felt like doing that, but people were counting on her there.

When she was at home, she immersed herself in any and all news she could get from the front, whether via print or film. She pored over every single news report, hoping to glean some information about what Ray's team might be doing, or where he might be.

If only she'd said something to him indicating that she wanted to hear from him. If only she had told him that she cared about what happened to him, he would have written or gotten in touch with her by now.

Ray had been counting on her. And she had let him down.

Suddenly Patsy felt her eyes fill with tears, and she was helpless to stop them. She turned away, hoping that Aunt Myrtle wouldn't notice.

But, of course, she did.

"Come now, Patsy dear. It can't be that bad," Myrtle said, her tone gentle, caring.

"Yes, it can." Patsy sniffed. She wiped her streaming eyes and scrubbed at her face with her hands, but all that did was make her feel worse. "Oh, Aunt Myrt, I've messed up. I've— I've screwed up so b-badly," she sobbed.

"Now, now, dear. Come to Aunt Myrtle and tell me all about it." She held open her arms and Patsy found herself being enveloped in a warm, comforting embrace. There was something so comforting about a warm hug from someone who cared, even if that someone wasn't Ray Darling.

RAY SAT LEANING AGAINST the hard bulkhead of the helicopter ferrying him to his destination and tried to catch some Zs. Some of the other guys were doing that, too, but so far, Ray hadn't been able to rest. Hell, he'd hardly slept since the last time he'd slept in Patsy's bed. Back when he'd believed nothing could tear them apart.

Since then, he'd lain awake at night battling with his ambivalent feelings about her. Should he be relieved that she didn't seem to care, or mad as hell? That couldn't have been Patsy at Base Ops. Surely he'd just been hallucinating. He leaned back again, feeling the vibrations of the powerful engines against his back, and tried to think above the drone of rotors.

He looked around and watched as one of the other guys scribbled a letter on a scrap of paper he'd taken from a pocket of his battle dress uniform. The airman had gotten a letter from his wife every time they'd had mail call. So far, Ray had received nothing. He'd even donated the one phone card he'd gotten in a USO packet to one of the guys who needed it more than he did.

Now, Ray wished he had it. He wanted to hear the sound of a familiar voice. More specifically, he wanted to hear Patsy's voice. If he couldn't touch her or hold her, he wanted at least to hear that she was okay. He wanted to talk to someone he loved.

But, no one who mattered knew where he was, much less, how to reach him.

Maybe he should write some letters, anyway. Maybe now was a good time to touch base with his parents once again. He'd tried for years to close the rift, and had finally given up. Maybe this was the right time to try again.

Hell, if he took the initiative to write a note to Patsy while he was at it, she might just take pity on him and drop him a line in return.

Ray reached over and nudged the airman on the arm. "Hey, Smith," he shouted to be heard through ear plugs used to cover the deafening engine noise. "Got a spare sheet of paper?"

PATSY HAD ALMOST decided not to stop at the mailbox when she came home that afternoon. It was raining so hard, she hadn't wanted to get any wetter than she already was from her dash from the clinic to her car. Though, deep inside, she knew she couldn't expect to hear from Ray, she kept hoping.

Though the rain had let up some, it hadn't stopped, so she quickly snatched the small pile of mail from the box to keep it from getting wet, then stuck it into her purse so it would stay dry. Patsy believed that as long as she didn't look through it right away, she could hold on to the hope that it would contain a letter. Once she looked, of course, that hope would be dashed.

Tripod greeted her at the door, barking. "What's the matter, doggie?" she asked as she hung her purse on the hook by the door and peeled out of her wet raincoat. "Are you hungry or just happy to see me?"

The dog had never been fond of storms, probably because the accident that had cost the dog her leg had happened during a storm, and this one was stronger than usual. As a clap of thunder crashed above them, Tripod yipped with fright and tore off, running down the hall.

Patsy sighed. She'd have to calm the dog down before she could tend to her own needs. The opportunity to slip into a nice warm, dry set of sweats was looking farther and farther away.

"Come, Tripod," Patsy called, coaxing the dog to her as she trudged down the short hall to her bedroom.

Once she had the dog calmed down and had dried herself off, she slipped into a comfortable, fleece sweat suit to banish the chill from the rain and the air conditioning inside.

Finally, the storm abated, and she fed Tripod, who ate her dinner with gusto, then turned her attention to a stuffed chew toy. Patsy heated up a microwave meal and carried it in to the living room. Only then did she think to look through the mail she'd left in her purse.

She sorted through the damp envelopes as she sat in front of the television set, her meal on the coffee table in front of her. With one eye on the screen and the other on the pile of mail, Patsy almost missed the small, grubby envelope near the bottom of the collection of circulars and junk mail. She looked closely at the return address on the envelope, then looked again, dropping her fork when she recognized the name scrawled nearly illegibly on the top line.

SSGT Raymond Darling!

She worked one trembling finger underneath the sealed envelope flap, careful not to tear through the return address.

Tears of joy filled her eyes as she read the letter inside.

Ray understood.

He knew what she was thinking and was right on the money. Oh, how she loved her Ray Darling.

And he loved her. He'd loved her for ages, but apparently had only realized how important it was to say the words to her when he saw her—*he saw her!*—the morning he left. He'd mouthed the words to her, but she hadn't caught that…

Her microwave dinner forgotten, she hurried to her desk for pen and paper.

She had to tell him just how much she loved him. He had to know for sure.

She had to explain and beg him for forgiveness.

RAY KNEW NOT TO EXPECT a response from any of his letters this soon, but he tried to guess when they might arrive. He also tried to imagine what the recipients would say, how they would react.

Would they respond at all?

He had to hope that they would.

In the meantime, his team had an important and dangerous job to do. He was suited up in desert survival gear, night-vision goggles at the ready, his parachute and pack strapped to him. This was going to be a big mission, and he didn't know what would happen, but at least, he'd done what he could to make peace with those he loved.

Just taking that first step, writing, had eased his mind, and he'd finally been able to get some restful sleep. Now, feeling refreshed and alert, he could be optimistic about both the mission at hand, and his future. It would all work out for the best.

He closed his eyes and tried to envision his homecoming.

Ray and the rest of his teammates waited impatiently as the big C-130 transport plane bringing them back to Hurlburt shut down its engines. Waiting for the signal that they could disembark, he looked toward the loadmaster.

Spouses and loved ones were not officially invited to the ramp when Special Operations teams returned from an operation, but usually someone figured out when they were due to arrive, and word went out through the "grapevine." The ramp was always crowded with loved ones waiting eagerly for glimpses of the returning servicemen and women.

He and the team still had to be debriefed and would have to stow their gear at the squadron, but just knowing that their loved ones were there waiting made it better.

Finally, the signal arrived and the crew opened the doors. Eagerly, the men filed to the door, one by one, cheerfully jostling and jockeying for position to be first to get outside.

Finally, he was on the ground. Ray scanned the jubilant congregation of people gathered in the shadows around the base operations building. One woman broke away from the crowd, apparently just as impatient and restless as the men on the team, and ran into her lover's arms. Then another. And another.

And suddenly, Patsy was there, grinning and laughing through tears of joy, her long blond hair blowing around her face in the night breeze. Ray opened his arms, and Patsy rushed to him, pressing her soft body against his chest, as he crushed her against him. If he had his way, he'd never let her go.

"I love you, Ray Darling," she whispered softly, shy in front of so many other people.

Hoo-ah, he cheered inwardly.

"I love you more, Patsy," Ray whispered around an enormous lump in his throat. Then their lips met and they kissed until Sergeant Scanlon interrupted it all too soon and called them to get their gear put away so they could be dismissed....

Ray smiled. He knew it was just a hope, a dream, but he had done his best to make it come true. If Patsy were even half the woman he hoped she was, he knew she'd be there when they finally came home.

"Why on earth are you standing there grinning like a fool, Sergeant?" Scanlon asked. "You sure you're up for this mission?"

"As ready as I'll ever be, Sergeant Scanlon," Ray replied.

"Well then, let's roll." The team leader turned to the assembled group of men and gave them the signal. "Load 'em."

THE LETTER FROM RAY had done a great deal to brighten Patsy's outlook, and she found that she wasn't quite as dependent on the newspaper and television for news of Ray.

Now, she could expect it in his own hand.

Once again, she hummed cheerfully as she performed her duties at the clinic. Everyone noticed, some people commented, and Patsy didn't mind at all.

One particularly busy morning, Patsy all but skipped into the clinic waiting room to call for the next patient, when she realized that every man and woman waiting there was riveted to the television set high on the wall. Patsy stopped short. "What's going on?"

"Quiet. Just listen," a sergeant with enough stripes to have authority told her tersely. So Patsy hushed and looked up at the screen.

"A detachment of special operations commandos, reported to be from Hurlburt Field, Florida, was ambushed in Taloom Kapoor last night," the announcer said. Footage of fighting, mostly flashes of light from guns firing against a dark green background seen through what must have been night-vision lenses, played on a screen behind him.

Patsy's heart nearly stopped beating and her legs went weak with the shock. She slumped into a chair. No, it couldn't be!

"Details are sketchy at this point, but though the unit was able to successfully defend themselves against the enemy, the number of casualties is extremely high,'' the announcer continued, his expression and tone appropriately somber.

The scene playing behind the man switched from battle footage to that of many wounded men being carried on stretchers to several waiting rescue helicopters. The faces of the attending medical personnel showed their concern, and that image told Patsy much more than what the announcer was saying.

Hardly daring to breathe, Patsy strained to see if she recognized the faces of any of the wounded, but the footage was too grainy and dark. Trembling, she pushed her heavy, nerveless body up out of the chair and stumbled back toward the examination rooms. She couldn't deal with this in front of everyone. She needed to be alone.

Mary Bailey caught up with her in the hall. ''Do you think someone you know is involved in that?'' she asked gently.

Numbly, Patsy nodded. ''Oh, Mary, I don't know what to do,'' she whispered, fighting to hold back tears.

''Someone you care about?''

''Yes, I love him,'' she confessed. ''And I never got the chance to tell him.''

Mary, older and more experienced in matters like this, took Patsy by the arms and made the younger woman look her square in the face. "People are counting on us to do our jobs here, and keeping yourself occupied will help you keep your mind off what's going on until we get more news," Mary told her firmly.

Wait? All she'd done for the past few weeks was wait. She'd finally admitted her feelings to herself and now Mary, as well as Ray, even if it was only on paper, and she didn't want to wait a moment longer.

She wanted Ray here. Safe with her. She wanted to hold him, to love him, to never let him go.

But she would do as Mary suggested.

She would keep herself busy.

And she would wait.

Chapter Twelve

Patsy performed her job at the clinic with the same quiet efficiency as she always had, but one tiny portion of her mind remained focused on any news she could get of Ray and his team.

One of the women she knew slightly had gotten a phone call from her husband telling her that he had been injured. She had been thrilled to know that he would be coming home soon.

Patsy had heard nothing.

Not a word.

She clung to the hope that she would get a telephone call, go home to find a message on her answering machine, a letter, anything that would assure her that Ray was alive. That he'd received her letter. That he would be coming home to her.

But days passed, and...nothing came.

All she could assume was that Ray was dead. And since Patsy was not a member of Ray Darling's family and since his family probably did not know about her because of their long estrangement from their son, she would likely never know exactly what had happened to the man she had realized too late she loved. Though Sergeant Hagarty had started that pool, and Ray's teammates obviously must have known about her, Patsy didn't think she could count on any of them to get word to her.

Patsy could only hope that when the rest of the team returned, she would hear about what had happened. But special operations personnel were notoriously close-mouthed about their missions, so she couldn't even count on that. She would eventually hear something about what had happened at Taloom Kapoor, but never the whole story, the real story. And she would never be certain that Ray had gotten her letter.

In the meantime, she had to go on. It had taken her many long months to pull herself out of the shock of losing her husband and family, but she didn't have that luxury now. She had an important job to do, as Mary had reminded her. She would do it.

When Mary came to her with a written order to send a nurse over on a transport plane going to Taloom Kapoor, Patsy leaped at the chance to go. Maybe someone there would know what had happened to Ray. Maybe she could find him. Maybe she could make it all right.

AFTER A LONG trans-Atlantic flight that included a stop at Lajes Air Base in the Azores for refueling, the plane finally landed at the temporary base one hundred miles south of Taloom Kapoor. Though Patsy had been able to walk around a little on the plane, and had even been allowed to get off the plane when it refueled, her legs were cramped and stiff from the long flight. She limped down the ladder from the plane to the ground and squinted in the brilliant sunshine. After the humidity of Florida, the arid heat of the desert was shocking to her system.

Patsy rubbed her dry and gritty eyes and tried to straighten out her aching limbs.

"Quite a change, isn't it?" Major Tewanda Hardy, the pilot, had climbed out of the plane and stood, surveying the rocky, treeless landscape.

"It looks so desolate," Patsy replied, glancing over at the tall, commanding woman she'd seen a few times around the base.

"It isn't exactly Florida, is it?" Major Hardy commented. "But what a boring world it would be if everything and everybody was exactly the same."

"I suppose you're right," Patsy agreed.

A woman in desert camouflage BDUs drove up

on a big-wheeled all-terrain vehicle that kicked up a cloud of dust and sand. She stopped, leaving the motor idling, climbed out and approached them. ''Is one of you Pritchard?''

Patsy nodded as one of those large human transport vehicles, a Humvee, pulled up next to a helicopter across the ramp.

''Well,'' Major Hardy said, smiling, ''you go do what you have to do, and I'll catch you on the return trip.'' Nodding to the newcomer, the major pivoted smartly, then strode away.

''Wow, was that Tewanda Hardy?''

''Sure. Why do you ask?''

''You don't know?'' The woman seemed incredulous that Patsy had seemed so nonplussed about chatting so casually with the major.

''That she's up for an air medal? Sure. She's a nice lady.''

Major Hardy was a much-honored and well-known female aviator, almost a legend around Hurlburt Field. She had flown her C-130 to where some special forces troops had been pinned down by the enemy, and had made a short-distance landing on the desert hardpan between the two opposing sides. The unexpected arrival of the plane had so startled their opponents that they had briefly forgotten to fire, allowing the Americans to get away. It had been a risky and gutsy move, and the major had been both reprimanded for her stunt and praised for her flying by her superiors.

The major had dismissed it as a bunch of unnecessary hoopla, supposedly telling the television bigwigs who had come calling that she was just a little girl from Huntsville, Alabama, who put her panty hose on one leg at a time like everyone else and didn't need all that attention.

Patsy admired her for her humility. As well as her heroics.

The corpsman, who was apparently there to escort her to the hospital, was still gawking at Major Hardy, so Patsy cleared her throat. "Don't we have something to do?"

"Oh, yeah," the corpsman said. She introduced herself and, looking appropriately embarrassed, went on. "I'm supposed to escort you to the hospital. Most of the guys are stable and won't need much care, but there are one or two who will need meds and dressing changes during the trip. We'll need to get you up to speed on their situations before you take off in the morning." She gestured for Patsy to climb into the all-terrain vehicle.

Still blinking in the brilliant afternoon sun, Patsy did so. Everything was happening so quickly, but perhaps now, she would be able to find out about Ray. Maybe he was one of the ones who needed special care.

She could only hope.

The airman prattled on about Major Hardy as she revved up the engine and Patsy glanced up at the dusty Humvee as they passed it. She could have sworn that one of the men in the cab looked a lot like Ray—he even wore dusty birth-control glasses—but that would have been too much of a coincidence. Patsy shook her head, then reached up to straighten her slouch hat. Her hair, pinned up for the trip, promptly tumbled down into her face. A gust of wind caught it and it flew around as though it had a mind of its own. As she fumbled to pin it back into place, she looked directly at the man who looked like Ray.

"It has to be wishful thinking," she told herself sternly as she attempted to secure the hat firmly on her head. It would be just too convenient for her to fly halfway around to world to find out any news about Sergeant Ray Darling and to have him drive by, apparently unharmed and safe and sound.

"You say something?"

"Oh, no." Holding her hat in place, she shook her head. "Just muttering to myself," she said and settled onto the seat beside her escort.

"Okay, fine," the woman said, and started off.

Then Patsy had her hands too full hanging on

for dear life as the vehicle bumped across the uneven terrain to wonder about the man she thought she'd seen.

"I MUST HAVE BEEN out in the desert way too long," Ray muttered, taking his glasses off and wiping them against the sleeve of his BDUs. He could have sworn he had just seen Patsy Pritchard climbing into an ATV. But that couldn't possibly be. Patsy was a civilian nurse safely back at home and working in the Flight Surgeon's Clinic at Hurlburt.

Still, he had to be sure. He placed his glasses, now only marginally cleaner than before, back on his nose and looked again through the window of the bouncing vehicle, which was kicking up an awful lot of dust, making it even harder to see. It certainly looked like her.

The woman was dressed in an obviously-new battle dress uniform still unfaded by the relentless sun, but the BDU appeared devoid of military rank or any service designation. He shrugged. She could be a reporter or some other civilian coming to observe.

Then the woman lifted her hand to shade her eyes and knocked her floppy camouflage hat off. Her flyaway mane shone in the bright desert sun like a gossamer web of flaxen silk, just like Patsy's. Time stood still as he stared at the waking dream in front of him. Then the woman grabbed at her hair and stuffed it up under the hat.

Ray shook his head to clear it of the imaginary image. Damn, he was seeing things.

The woman looked up and, for just an instant, their eyes met. If it wasn't Patsy, why did he feel as if the breath had been knocked out of him?

The waiting helicopter, fueled and ready to take them on another of an endless string of reconnaissance missions, started up and Ray climbed aboard. He didn't have time to think about what he'd seen.

Besides, it was ludicrous to think that Patsy Pritchard was out here in the desert.

It had to be some sort of mirage. Or daydream. It was simply wishful thinking resulting from loneliness and too many days and nights sleeping in a tent out in the desert.

It damn sure couldn't be real.

WHILE SHE WAITED for her patients to be prepped for transport, Patsy wandered through the hospital in Taloom Kapoor, but she saw not one familiar face. She strained to recognize anyone through burns and bandages and sunburns and razor stubble. Not one of the wounded was Ray. And no one seemed able to tell her what had happened to one SSGT Ray Darling. It was as if he had vanished from the face of the earth.

She had to find out something, to glean some tiny little fact that would tell her that he was alive. Or dead. Anything.

Then one, last, desperate idea came to her. There was one other person who might be able to give her the information she needed. Patsy approached the charge nurse who had performed triage the night the casualties had come in.

Colonel Clark was an experienced service-woman, sturdy and no-nonsense, but with the warm eyes of one who truly cared about her patients. Patsy hoped that meant she would bend a regulation or two to give her the information she needed. "Can you tell me the names of the men who were killed in the Taloom Kapoor incident?" she asked, laying her question right out on the table.

"You know I can't tell you that," the colonel said. "But, maybe if you rephrase your question, I might be able to tell you something."

With that suggestion, Patsy's hopes were raised. She thought about it. "Well, if I give you a name could you tell me if he has been a patient here in any capacity? If you've seen or heard of him?"

"Maybe. I can't remember every name attached to every splinter or stomachache that walked in here, but I remember the special ones."

The seriously injured and the ones you couldn't help, Patsy thought but didn't say.

Patsy swallowed. It was now or never. "All right," she said, then drew a deep breath and moistened her lips, stalling lest the answer be one she didn't want. "Do you remember Sergeant Ray Darling?" She hardly dared to breathe as she waited for the colonel's answer.

The no-nonsense look left the woman's face, and she broke into a smile that feathered lines around her eyes. They sparkled and gave her a beauty Patsy hadn't recognized a moment before. "No, Patsy. I can honestly say that I haven't seen your Sergeant Darling in any capacity here," she said. "I'd certainly remember a name like that."

Patsy could have whooped for joy. Instead, she impulsively hugged the older nurse and was rewarded with a warm hug in return. "Thank you," she whispered, her voice husky with emotion. "Thank you."

The colonel, still smiling, shrugged. "I didn't do anything."

"Yes, you did," Patsy insisted. "You relieved a very worried mind."

RAY CLIMBED BACK onto the helicopter after another successful mission. Though he'd kept his attention focused on the job at hand, he hadn't been able to get the image of the blond woman in the battle dress uniform out of his mind. He knew it could not have been Patsy, but it had seemed so real, he couldn't dismiss it.

Could Patsy be in Taloom Kapoor?

And if she was there, *why* was she there?

Could it be that she had come all the way out here looking for him?

He had to get back to base. He had to find her. Talk to her, kiss her, hold her in his arms.

No, he told himself. It was too much to dream that Patsy had come all the way here for him, yet he couldn't help feeling that she was near.

On the other hand, he had yet to receive a response from her after he'd poured his heart out to her on paper. He'd hoped for a letter in return. His parents had already responded to their letter, and he was looking forward to a reunion with them when this deployment was over.

Nothing, however, had come from Patsy: not a letter, not a postcard, not a word. He was quite certain now that he *hadn't* really seen her watching in the shadows of Base Ops when they'd taken off. And if the woman he'd thought was Patsy had really been someone else, then...

The reason Patsy had not told him she loved him was because she didn't.

Patsy didn't care.

And that certainly hadn't been Patsy he'd thought he'd seen getting on that ATV back at camp.

THE TRANSPORT TAKING the injured stateside had been scheduled to leave far too early for Patsy's taste, especially since the shock of traveling halfway across the world had yet to wear off. Even with the mandatory crew rest period, she had barely had time to adjust to the time difference, and now they were about to head back to Hurlburt Field.

It amazed and awed her how cold and dark it was at night in the desert when it had been so unbearably hot the day before, and she stared up at a sky dusted with more stars than she'd ever seen before. Patsy recognized some of the familiar constellations, yet there were other stars in the desert sky, stars that shone too dimly to be seen through the milky, humid, night air on the Gulf Coast of Florida.

Still, she wasn't particularly interested in stargazing. Patsy still hoped she might happen to see Ray. The chances of her finding him were next to none now, but she had clung so fiercely to the hope that their paths might intersect that she was unwilling to give up looking until she was actually secured into the C-130 and airborne.

And she *had* seen that man who looked remarkably like Ray going by in that Humvee when she'd first arrived, she reminded herself almost hourly. Patsy wasn't convinced that the man was Ray, but neither had she been shown that he wasn't. She'd been bundled off to the hospital before she'd gotten a good look.

Whoever the man was, he had to be away on a mission because he had climbed into a helicopter waiting on the pad. There was still a slight chance that the helicopter and its crew would return before she left....

No sooner had she thought it then the quiet solitude of midnight was shattered by the roar of a big helicopter's powerful engine. The chilly air which had been still and calm, suddenly whipped about as if it were trying to emulate a hurricane, or maybe a tornado. Dust swirled around her, and she closed her eyes to protect them from the grit and sand.

The rumble of the engine wound down, and the force of the wind decreased as the huge rotors slowed. Patsy opened her eyes as a squad of men, so heavily laden with gear that it was impossible to recognize anyone, climbed off the helicopter.

Something in her told her that one of those men was Ray. She could feel his presence. She knew he was there, felt it in her heart, but it would be so much better to see him, to touch him, to hold him in her arms, if only for a moment. To know for sure. Her heart raced and her breath caught in her throat in anticipation of seeing his darling face.

One man paused and, for just a moment, looked across the ramp toward the hulking transport plane

Patsy was about to board. For a moment, he seemed to focus on her. Patsy started to wave, and actually lifted her hand to do so, but someone called to her. Reluctantly, she turned away to see what the intruder wanted.

"We need to be wheels up before the sun," a crew chief called to her. "Waiting on you."

"Okay, sure," Patsy said, reluctantly following the man to the ladderlike steps. She managed one last glance over her shoulder, but the man—no, Ray, it had to be!—was now lost in the crowd of similarly dressed servicemen boarding another Humvee. Still, she waved. She had to take the chance that he'd see her.

Ray might not see her. He might not even be there, but Patsy's heart had sensed that he was.

She stepped inside and the loadmaster closed and secured the door.

"GET THE LEAD OUT, Radar!" Sergeant Scanlon shouted as they hustled to offload their equipment so they could head back out to their quarters and get some sleep. But Ray had fixed his vision on the slight form standing near the C-130 across the ramp. The ground crew was busy readying the transport for departure, but this solitary figure stood idle.

He stared at her as hard as he could, and she

seemed to respond to his mental message and turned toward him. Even this far away, Ray felt as though they were connected. As if their souls had touched.

It had to be Patsy. He could feel it in his heart. His loins tightened in recognition, but what could Patsy be doing over here? And why hadn't she tried to see him?

Instead of waving, or in some way acknowledging that she'd seen him, the woman looked away.

What did that mean? Did she not recognize him? Did she not know him at all? Or, worse, had she telegraphed her true feelings to him by turning her back to him when he was at his most vulnerable? Damn, he wished he could speak to her.

"Darling!" the Sergeant yelled again, and Ray knew better than to take exception this time. He had a job to do, even if the immediate mission was over. He was holding everybody else up. He had no business mooning over some strange woman, even if she looked a little like Patsy Pritchard.

No, not a little. A lot.

He returned to stowing his equipment on the Humvee and grabbed a handhold with which to swing himself up and into the vehicle. The engines on the C-130 hadn't started up yet, so the woman might still be there watching. Ray strained for one last look, but the Humvee jerked into motion. Then he was too busy hanging on to look any more.

She could just as easily have been a perfect stranger, he tried to tell himself. She was not necessarily the woman he loved showing him in no uncertain terms that she didn't share his feelings....

Chapter Thirteen

Buoyed by the knowledge that Ray had been unharmed by the ambush at Taloom Kapoor, Patsy
threw herself cheerfully into her work once she returned. She gave herself daily—no, hourly—pep
talks with reasons why Ray had not responded to
her heartfelt letter. He *was* stationed at a temporary
post in a faraway country, for example, and mail
delivery was probably sporadic, at best.

After six weeks that had seemed to Patsy more
like six years, the deployment of the special operations team from Hurlburt came to an end. She saw
men wearing the familiar scarlet berets everywhere
around the base, and several of the men she had
escorted back to Hurlburt had already returned to
active duty. It would only be a matter of time before
she could expect to hear from Ray. Before they'd
finally be together again.

Patsy lived for that reunion, but two more, long weeks passed and still she didn't hear from him.

She wanted to believe that nothing was wrong, but her cheerful optimism was gradually fading.

Mary Bailey noticed that her once buoyant spirits had taken a downward turn. "What's up, Patsy?" she asked one day in a concerned tone.

It was all Patsy could do to keep from crying. "I haven't heard one word from my boyfriend since the team got back. He's not returning my calls to his apartment. I even called the section and they took a message for him, so I'm assuming he's around, he's just not interested in calling me back."

Mary folded Patsy into a warm hug. "Don't jump to conclusions, Patsy. He might not have gotten the message, and a lot of the single guys have taken leave to visit their families. You know, to assure their mothers and fathers that they're all right."

"Y-you think?" Patsy asked, her lip quivering in spite of her attempts to remain in control.

"Sure. What else could it be?" the older woman said more confidently than Patsy felt. "Think positive."

"I'll try," Patsy said, then she remembered something that Mary didn't know. Ray had been estranged from his family for years. It wasn't likely that he'd be visiting them. They probably didn't even know that he'd been over in the desert.

Then she went home and found the letter she'd written to Ray in her mailbox, marked "Return to Sender." It seemed that her worst fears had been confirmed.

RAY TRIED TO ENJOY his reunion with his family, but the fact that he hadn't heard from Patsy still worried him. He'd poured his heart out to her in that letter. Not even the coldest witch would have been able to ignore it. Yet, Patsy had.

At least his letter to his family had hit the target. He'd received several letters and cards from his parents while he was still in the desert assuring him that they loved him and wanted to see him. So when he'd been granted leave after returning to Hurlburt, he'd taken the opportunity to go home for the first time in ten years.

He sighed.

"What's wrong, son?" Janet Darling asked. "Are you tired of us already?"

Ray forced himself to grin. "Not for a minute, Mom." It was the truth. He was grateful that his deployment had provided the opportunity for him to mend fences with his family, but his joy at being home was tempered by Prickly Pritchard's betrayal. Obviously, she didn't care for him. Why else would she not have bothered to respond to his letter? "It's been great to be back at home with you and Dad, but there's somebody back in Florida."

"A woman somebody?" his mother asked, her eyes lighting up with interest.

"Yeah," Ray said, punctuating his reply with a sigh. "At least, I thought there was. Now I'm not so sure."

PATSY HAD GIVEN UP hope of hearing from Ray. She had to face that he'd lost interest in her. Obviously, he didn't know that she'd written back to him. No wonder he hadn't tried to get in touch with her.

She tried to convince herself that knowing Ray had been a good thing. He had finally helped her get over the hurdle of dating again. She could always go out with one of those men Aunt Myrtle was always trying to fix her up with. Patsy thought about that and grimaced.

"What's the funny face for?" Nancy Oakley, back from maternity leave, asked.

Patsy chuckled. "I was thinking about the type of guy my aunt was likely to set me up with."

Nancy laughed. "Oh yeah, I can see him now, Pat. Some smart accountant type with lots of brains and thick, black-rimmed glasses," Nancy said.

Patsy didn't laugh. Nancy didn't know how close

her description had been to the last man that Aunt Myrtle had fixed her up with. He wasn't an accountant, but the brains and the glasses were right on.

HE'D BEEN ACCEPTED for Officer Training School!

Ray felt like cheering most of the time. Except when he thought about Patsy Pritchard.

When he received the notice that he'd been accepted to OTS, he had whooped for joy. The rest of the guys in the squadron had hoo-ahed right along with him. Being accepted to OTS was the only thing that had kept him sane after being dumped. Sure, he was still disappointed in Patsy, but he'd get over it.

He hoped.

OTS would keep him busy and definitely keep his mind off her. And it would take him away from the possibility of running into her every day on the base. Now, he could understand why Danny had been in such a foul mood since his auction date, and he'd only been out with the woman once.

He just had to get through the physical exam before reporting to Maxwell Air Force Base in Alabama for the training. He waited, impatiently drumming his fingers against the plastic waiting room chair next to him, in the Flight Surgeon's Office. He wasn't worried about the physical. He and the rest of the guys in the squadron were in tip-top shape.

He *was* worried that he would run into Patsy Pritchard. But so far, he hadn't seen her. Ray checked his watch. Dr. Brantley must be running behind. Ray sure hoped he'd call him soon. The longer he lingered in this waiting room, the more likely he was to encounter Patsy.

And he wasn't sure what he'd do if he did.

PATSY PLUCKED the thick medical file off the pile on the counter behind the reception desk and glanced at the name. Then she did a double take. She blinked, shook her head, and looked at it again. No, it couldn't be.

It had to be an hallucination. There was no way she could really be looking at the medical records for Staff Sergeant Ray Darling. Fate wouldn't be so cruel as to taunt her like that....

Apparently, it *was* that cruel, and this *was* real. She actually had to take the man's vitals and record them in his file.

Taking a deep breath, she stepped into the waiting room doorway and started to call Ray's name. But she found she couldn't speak. She swallowed an enormous lump of emotion, cleared her throat and called him again. Her voice sound strangled and strange, even to her.

Ray started to push himself up out of the plastic waiting room chair, but upon seeing her he paused. His eyes brightened with recognition, then the happy look disappeared behind shuttered eyes, and he straightened, affecting a somber expression as he came toward her.

"Nurse Pritchard," he said curtly.

Patsy's heart sank. He *was* angry with her. "Follow me," she managed as she tried to think what might bring him around. "I have to take your vitals, although, you look wonderful, so I don't know why I need to." She managed a bright smile in spite of the cloudy expression on Ray's face. "I'm so happy you made it back all in one piece."

"Thanks," he muttered.

Though Patsy wanted to throw her arms around Ray and kiss him senseless, she forced herself to remain at a safe distance from him. She directed him to the screening nook and pulled a curtain across the opening to protect them from prying eyes.

"Is that necessary?" he asked, his voice still hard and cold.

"Ray, you have to listen to me," Patsy pleaded. "Please."

He started to walk out.

She grabbed his arm, and he stopped. Keeping

his back to her, he looked over his shoulder, one eyebrow raised in question.

''I did answer your letter. I really did. It was returned by the post office.''

Ray rolled his eyes. ''Yeah, right. That's convenient, Pritchard. Can you prove it?''

Patsy's breath caught in her throat. Lord help her, she could. ''Yes,'' she said, breathless with excitement. ''As a matter of fact, I can. Wait here.''

Praying silently that Ray would wait, Patsy darted out of the cubicle and hurried to her desk to get the purse she'd stashed in the bottom drawer. Why she'd kept that letter, she didn't know. And why she had put it in her purse and actually had it with her today was even more unfathomable.

But she had it with her. Maybe she had hoped for an opportunity just like this. No matter what the reason, she had the proof she needed to show Ray that she really did care. She snatched her bag from the bottom desk drawer and, rummaging in the depths for the letter, she hurried back to Ray.

He was still there, his jaw clenched firmly, a muscle twitching ominously under one eye.

She handed him the unopened letter, marked ''Return to Sender,'' and waited.

He took it gingerly, holding it with two fingers, and examined the letter as though it were an ancient papyrus there to be authenticated by experts. "It's still sealed," he said, his tone questioning.

"I didn't need to open it," Patsy said simply. "I know what I wrote in it."

"Why did you keep it?"

Patsy didn't really know. Not consciously, at least. She just had. All she knew is that though she'd taken it to the trash can more than once, she hadn't been able to throw it away. "It just seemed important to keep it," she said, her heart lodged in her throat.

Ray continued to examine the sealed envelope.

"Open it, Ray. It's the only way you'll believe me," Patsy urged. "I do love you. I've loved you almost from that moment you first flirted with me in this very treatment room. I'm sorry I gave you reason to doubt it."

He looked up quickly, hope flaring briefly in his eyes behind the lenses of his dear, familiar BC glasses. But he said nothing.

"Darn it, Ray. I went all the way to Taloom Kapoor to try to find you. You have to believe me!"

He jerked his head up to look at her. "So it really was you!"

"Yes, I was there. I thought I saw you, but you were going away as I was coming in."

"And I was coming back as you were going away," Ray concluded. He drew in a deep breath, then detached his government issue knife from the lanyard attached to his belt, slid it under the flap and slit the envelope open. Patsy held her breath as he read.

Please let him understand, Patsy prayed silently. *He has to believe me.*

His expression lightening with every page he read, Ray finally looked up, his eyes bright, his cheeks creased with a broad grin. "You do love me."

"Of course I do," Patsy replied.

"But like I said in the letter, I was terrified that if I voiced the words out loud, it would become so much more real. As long as you didn't know, then we'd be okay." Patsy looked away, embarrassed at voicing the sentiment that sounded exceedingly silly, now that she'd said it. "I didn't want you to die like my parents. Like Ace and the kids. Silly, huh?" she said, turning.

"No, not silly at all," Ray said, folding the letter and returning it to the envelope. He stuffed it into his pocket and took her hands. "I think I understand. And I'm sorry, once again, for not telling you how I felt earlier. I've never been in love before."

As he closed his strong, capable hands over hers, Patsy's heart swelled with joy. She knew everything was going to be all right. She leaned toward him for a kiss.

''Where's my next patient?'' Dr. Brantley called, and Ray and Patsy quickly stepped apart.

''I haven't taken your vitals, and your blood pressure will probably be through the roof,'' Patsy said, groaning.

''Yeah.'' Ray opened the curtain. ''But somebody else can record it later, after it has a chance to go down.''

Patsy stepped back. ''What are you here for, anyway? You're not sick, are you?'' She handed him his file.

''No, I got accepted for OTS. This is the physical for it.''

''Oh, no. This encounter could cost you your slot if your pressure doesn't go down!''

''No, Brantley will understand, and he'll let me wait until I've calmed down.''

Patsy had to hope that Ray was right. If he wasn't she'd move Heaven and Earth to convince the doctor that it had been her fault that Ray had failed.

Ray winked at Patsy. ''Wish me luck.''

''You've got it,'' Patsy said, watching him confidently stride away.

Then she whispered a little prayer and went to look for her next patient.

''Hoo-ah!'' Ray cheered. ''Thanks,'' he said. ''Now, I've got to go tell my girl.''

Without waiting for a response, Ray strode down the quiet corridor to where Patsy was straightening supplies in a cabinet, grabbed her from behind and swung her into his arms.

Startled, she gasped, but then Patsy looked up at his jubilant face, and she broke into a brilliant smile. "Did you?"

"I did."

"But nobody took your vitals. The doctor didn't fudge them, did he?"

"Silly, silly, Patsy," Ray said, holding her closer and tipping her chin up so he could look into her clear blue eyes. "Dr. Brantley said he wouldn't let you within a mile of me until after Nurse Bailey took my pressure. He wanted me to pass as much as I did."

He glanced back over his shoulder to where Mary Bailey and Doctor Brantley stood, beaming, seeming as happy about their reunion as he was.

"Then it's final?" Patsy asked. "You passed? You're going to Officer Training School? When?"

"Next month," Ray said. "I just need to know one thing."

"What?"

"Do you want to get married before I report to OTS or after?"

Patsy's eyes grew wide with surprise. "Sergeant Darling, is that a proposal?"

"Yeah, I guess it is," he whispered, his voice strangely thick.

Patsy blushed, her fair skin glowing with love. "Do you suppose you could do it in the good, old-fashioned way?"

"Like on bended knee?"

"No, not exactly. I hate to be difficult, but a woman doesn't get asked that question very often. I'd like to actually hear the words."

"In front of witnesses?" Ray grinned and glanced over his shoulders toward the doctor and nurse who weren't even pretending to ignore what was going on.

"Ask me, Ray," Patsy demanded impatiently. "I can't wait to give you my answer."

Ray grinned. "Aha! That must mean yes."

"Ra-ay! Don't keep me waiting forever."

"Wouldn't dream of it," Ray said with a grin. Then lowered himself to the floor. Kneeling in front of her, Ray took Patsy's hands. Her skin was soft and silky and so delicate and white against his coarse, tanned hand. He imagined how her third finger, left hand, would look wearing his ring.

He cleared his throat. "Patsy Pritchard, I love you. Would you do me the honor of becoming my wife?"

Though he was pretty sure he knew what the answer would be, Ray held his breath.

Patsy smiled softly and her eyes glistened with tears. Her mouth worked, but she couldn't seem to make any sound come out.

"Please, Patsy. You're killing me here," Ray pleaded, looking up into her brimming eyes.

She swallowed and moistened her lips, then, nodding vigorously so that there could be no doubt, she whispered the words he so eagerly wanted to hear. "Yes, Ray. Yes. I will marry you. I will be your wife."

Ray pulled her down into his arms and kissed her, tenderly at first, then he deepened the kiss. Nothing mattered but the beautiful, caring woman he was holding in his arms. Not even the doctor and nurse and Nancy Oakley, who'd come to investigate the noise, and who were now cheering as loudly as the spectators at any NFL game, or the smiles and applause of everyone else in the clinic.

Finally, Ray ended the kiss. He climbed to his feet and reached down to Patsy, feeling a thrill of excitement when she took his hand. He felt as though he were standing on top of the world, as though he could leap over tall buildings. He had softened Prickly Pritchard. He felt as though he could do anything. Would he ever stop feeling like this? He hoped not.

He helped Patsy, still smiling crookedly through her tears, to her feet and positioned her in front of

him. "I asked you another question before, Patsy."
He swallowed and cleared his throat. "When will
it be? Before or after I go to OTS?"

Patsy swallowed a sob and wiped her streaming
eyes with trembling hands, and Mary offered her a
tissue. She wiped again, blotting away the tears.
Ray wanted to shake the answer out of her, but he
knew she'd tell him in her own time.

Finally, Patsy cleared her throat. "Nothing would
make me happier than to become your wife yesterday, Ray Darling, but I think we should wait until
after you graduate from OTS." She smiled another
one of those endearing, lopsided smiles. "Aunt
Myrtle would never forgive me if I cheated her out
of planning this wedding. Will you mind very much
waiting?"

Ray smiled and shook his head. "No, Patsy. I
owe your aunt a lot. After all, she was the one who
brought us together by buying my services at that
bachelor auction. No, I don't mind. Just as long as
it isn't too long after I graduate," he clarified.

"Don't you worry, Ray Darling," Patsy replied
with a grin. "I'm not the kind of girl who goes for
long engagements. I can't wait to become a Darling
just like you."

Ray, who usually had something to say about
everything, was at a loss for words.

"Hoo-ah," he finally managed. "You are a Darling now. As far as I'm concerned, you always have been."

"Hoo-ah," Patsy echoed.

Epilogue

Fifteen months later

Patsy Darling, still tired, but elated from giving birth, gazed lovingly down at the two tiny bundles in her arms, one wrapped in pink, the other in blue, and smiled. It was all she could do not to explode from happiness, her heart was so full of love and emotion for this double blessing she'd been given.

The door to the hospital room creaked open and Ray, grinning broadly, peered inside. "Hello, family," he said. "Are you ready for some other visitors?"

"I'm ready for the media," Patsy said, her soft smile changing to a grin of her own. "I happen to have the two most beautiful babies in the world, and I want everyone to know it."

Janet Darling stepped into the room. "Oh, they will. If Ray has anything to say about it. That son of mine has passed out bubble gum cigars to every single person who's had the misfortune to cross his path since he picked us up at the airport.''

Ray shrugged. ''They didn't seem to mind. And I still have plenty more.''

''Heaven help us,'' Patsy murmured.

Raymond Darling Senior followed his wife into the room. ''Sure are small,'' he said gruffly, but Patsy could tell that he was doing all he could to disguise the overwhelming emotion he felt. As much as he and Ray protested it, they were so much alike it was uncanny, right down to the identical reactions they'd both had when they'd gotten their first looks at the twins.

''Do you want to hold them, Grandma and Grandpa?'' Patsy lifted the boy toward Grandma Janet who leaned in to take him. She balanced him comfortably into the crook of her arm.

Ray's father reached for the other baby, gingerly picking up the pink bundle of joy. He held her carefully away from him as though she were a bomb about to explode. ''Hello, little one,'' he whispered, his voice thick, his expression goofy with unconditional love. Then he shifted her closer and held her against his heart. ''I'm your Grandpa.''

The baby wriggled and waved her arms reflexively, and Raymond touched a finger to her tiny hand. He grinned when her little fingers closed around it. ''Look how strong she is!''

"That's my daughter," Ray said, chest swelling with pride.

"Your son's a real charmer, too," Janet said as the baby yawned and stretched as though he were accustomed to all the attention. "Don't forget him."

"How could I? I still can't believe we ended up with two babies for the price of one."

"I don't know why, Ray," Patsy said. "We had several months to get used to the idea."

"But it wasn't real until they were actually here," Ray said.

Suddenly, the hospital door flew open and one more visitor burst in, looking like a bouquet of fresh flowers in a brightly colored pantsuit next to Ray in his drab uniform, and his parents, in conservative grays. "Do my great-grandniece and nephew have names yet?" Aunt Myrtle demanded without preamble.

"They are almost twenty-four hours old and they are still nameless!" She fluttered to a halt at the foot of the hospital bed and looked from baby to baby in the Darlings' arms.

"Hello," she said. "I'm Myrtle Carter, Patsy's great aunt."

As if there could be any doubt, Patsy thought with a chuckle. "Aunt Myrtle, these are Ray's parents: Janet and Raymond Darling."

"Charmed," Myrtle said, not removing her gaze from the babies. "Well, as I said, I can't call them boy and girl. And it isn't as if I have forever to wait to learn their names."

"Aunt Myrtle, you *will* be around forever," Patsy said, meaning it.

Ray chuckled. "Patsy and I never really had a chance to settle on names since they came three weeks early, but I got to thinking about it in the car on the way to pick up my folks at the airport."

"Oh?" Patsy asked, wondering if she should be miffed at not being consulted.

"I was thinking about Carter and Janet," Ray said softly. "How about Carter Raymond and Janet Myrtle? That way they'll be named for both our families. After Myrtle for bringing us together and for my parents because if it weren't for them, I wouldn't be here in the first place. What do you think?"

Patsy's heart swelled and her eyes filled with tears. It was obvious that Aunt Myrtle and Janet were thrilled with the suggestion, too. Smiles of pleasure crossed each face. "Let me hold my babies," Patsy whispered.

Ray frowned as his parents passed the twins over to their mother. "Does that mean you don't want to use those names?"

Patsy shook her head as she settled the babies

into her arms. Then, her heart overflowing with love, she looked down at them. "Hello, Carter and Jannie," she whispered, her voice thick with emotion. She kissed each baby on the top of its fuzzy head. "I'm your mother."

Aunt Myrtle clapped her hands, bangle bracelets on her wrists jangling. "Wonderful. What perfect names for two perfect little babies." She swooped in to hover over them. "Hello, little ones. I'm your Aunt Myrtle. If it hadn't been for me," she twittered proudly, "you wouldn't be here."

Janet and Raymond Darling looked at each other with questioning expressions.

"It's a long story, Mom, Dad."

"No, it isn't," Aunt Myrtle protested. "I purchased your son at a charity bachelor auction and gave him to my niece."

"And then you all lived happily ever after?" Janet asked.

"Not exactly, Mom, but we will from now on," Ray replied. "We ran into a few bumps along the way," he explained.

"But it all worked out for the best," Patsy agreed. "And we certainly will be happy from now on and forever."

"Yes, they will," Aunt Myrtle agreed. "I wouldn't have it any other way."

"Hoo-ah," Ray said.

Coming soon from

HARLEQUIN®

AMERICAN *Romance*®

Cowboys BY THE DOZEN!

by

TINA LEONARD

The Jefferson brothers of Malfunction Junction,
Texas, know how to lasso a lady's heart—
and then let it go without a ruckus.

But these twelve rowdy ranchers are in for the
ride of their lives when the local ladies begin
rounding up hearts and domesticating
cowboys...by the dozen.

Don't miss—
FRISCO JOE'S FIANCÉE (HAR #977)
available 7/03

LAREDO'S SASSY SWEETHEART (HAR #981)
available 8/03

RANGER'S WILD WOMAN (HAR #986)
available 9/03

TEX TIMES TEN (HAR #989)
available 10/03

*Available at your favorite retail outlet.
Only from Harlequin Books!*

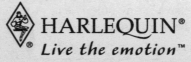

HARLEQUIN®
Live the emotion™

Visit us at www.americanromances.com

HARCBTD

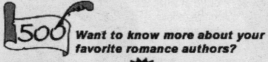

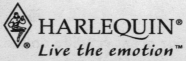

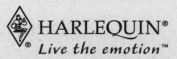

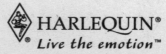